TELECOMMUTING

L. MARIE WOOD

Copyright© 2020 L. Marie Wood

Trade Paperback ISBN: 978-1-7371320-0-4

Cover Art by Maya Preisler

Editor: Nicole Givens Kurtz

Proofreader: Alexandra Christian

Publisher: Mocha Memoirs Press

Author's Note

ONE

C amera working? Check.
      Hair is combed.
Tie is straight.

No sleep in my eyes, boogers in my nose, or general shit on my face.

What *is* sleep anyway? Or that white shit that gathers in the corners of your mouth when you're talking, stretching and pulling each time you open your lips wide, blowing in the breeze that is your breath, just enough for the other person to see...

Headset? Check, though damn if it doesn't make me look like a DJ from the 80s. Or an air traffic controller with those huge, padded ear cushions and the stick microphone in front of my mouth.

Pen and paper on the desk in front of me to make it look like I truly give a shit about what the guy on the other side says about reporting structure, responsibilities, customer satisfaction, yadda yadda? You bet, sir. Right you are. Absolutely. Yeah, suck my dick.

Is the camera on?

Check.

My sigh was loud in the quiet room. Every damned thing is loud now because the house is so fucking empty. Four bedrooms, 2.5 baths, carpet and hardwood floors, three levels; rooms that will stay empty because it's just me in here now... me, myself, and I.

This is too much space for one person. There are too many places that will go unused, unvisited, uninhabited. But now's not the time to think about that, is it? Now isn't the time to think about how she walked out nearly a week ago taking most of her shit with her - that was easy to do since almost all of it was still packed in boxes anyway because we just fucking moved in here - taking all the sun and the light and the goddamned air with her.

No, now is the time to think about the interview, not that shit. That shit will be there waiting for me once the interview is over. I'm sure of that.

The interview that would start in about 2 minutes.

The interview I set up a month ago when everything was peachy. The one that had gotten pushed because some bigwig had business overseas and it was all hands on deck or some shit.

The one for the job that I really need.

Yeah, I need this job and its sizeable paycheck because I have to pay this big-assed mortgage by myself now... at least until I can sell it. I need this job because I'm too tired of looking to stay out in the job market if I don't have to. I need this job, even though the perk of working from home, the one where I thought I might be able to go upstairs and sleep with my fiancée before my 10 o'clock meeting every day, didn't matter much anymore because she was gone, ancient history, ghost, Audi 5000 – maybe I'm a 1980s DJ stuck in a future I don't like the look of.

Back to the future.

Can I go back? Not too far. Maybe just a few months. Shit, I'll take a couple days. Maybe I could kiss her before she says she's done, apologize before she packs her bags.

Maybe.

Microphone? Microphone check? *A one, two... a one, two.* DJ, rapper... it's all the same thing.

I smile my best fake smile and stop as quickly as I started. My teeth looked too long reflected on my computer monitor (again, yes, the camera is on and working – stop worrying about that!). Too predatory. Like a wolf.

I laugh because didn't she say I was like a chameleon? Always changing, so much so that she never knew who she was going to get from day to day? Didn't werewolves change with the full moon? Didn't werewolves have sharp teeth?

Werewolves. I'm a werewolf. Not a fucking lizard.

I laugh again, then cringe.

Some laugh. More like a bark.

I clear my throat, trying to break up the phlegm that has gathered there from disuse.

I haven't spoken a word since she walked out that door.

"Hello, my name is..." I practiced.

There had been no yelling, no begging, no leaving 50 voicemails so she and her friends could call me a stalker. After the door to our new, too dammed big for one person house shut, my mouth shut. There nothing left to say anyway.

I cleared my throat again. So scratchy... hardly sound like myself at all.

"Thanks for the opportunity to speak with you about..."

Jacket...? Damn it, where's my suit jacket?

One minute left.

Fuck.

Do I really need the jacket?

Where the fuck *is* the jacket?

I look too plain.

Plain, blending in with the taupe (tan, beige, khaki, fucking wheat... whatever) wall behind me.

Indistinguishably lighter version of brown wall.

Off-white shirt.

Forgettable tie.

Skin in need of sun.

Hollow eyes.

Shit, I need that jacket.

Is it still packed away in a box?

Is my midnight blue jacket still in an unpacked box upstairs, balled up and wrinkled because that's how I packed my clothes because some parts of adulting still allude me? No. I remember navigating the boxes of crap strewn around the bedroom to find it. I slept against the one labeled 'Closet' last night, so I should know.

Some of her dresses are still in there.

We hadn't even really unpacked all the way. We just fucking got here a few weeks ago and she was gone already, gone to greener pastures, gone to somewhere, maybe even some*one* else.

That bitch.

Nah, I know better.

If I was gonna go back in time, a couple days wouldn't cut it.

Not by a long shot.

I stood to scan the foyer for my jacket. Fucking house is big enough to have a real foyer, not just a landing between two stairwells, some rectangular space barely big enough to hold three full grown adults unless one of them didn't mind ducking into the closet bordering it. A real fucking foyer. And she was already gone.

There. On the floor. In the foyer.

The jacket.

Computer ringing... ha, I'm gonna *love* this. Fucking obnoxious already.

I run to grab my jacket because why not.

My sweatpants were old. They're not those new type of ones that grip at the ankle – joggers, or whatever. They're old fashioned, loose-fitting sweats that nobody looks cool in... and they have a hole in them right where the knee bends, making the hole spread wide when I sit, and gape like a mouth when I stand. I hope I don't forget about it and stand up during the interview, play an impromptu game of 'Peek-A-Boo' with the interviewing committee – yeah, that'll really score me some points. Note to self – keep your ass in the seat.

Why the hell did it have to be a video interview anyway?

Deep breath.

Calm the fuck down.

The jacket's a bit snug but it'll do. It'll have to.

Second ring...

I look better this way – a little color, a little style. She always said so... and she was right.

Third ring...

Funny that the ringer on the computer sounds like the one that cordless landlines used to use... but not quite.

Fourth ring...

Smooth my hair, practice that fake smile once more, this time with less teeth.

Fifth ri-

Three people sitting around a conference table, looking at me expectantly.

Here we go.

"Hello! Thank you so much for the opportunity to interview..."

TWO

O k. Computer delivered today. Big-assed box with a laptop, mouse, and a monitor.

Got a notification that another shipment is coming later today. Probably my cellphone.

This shit is real now.

Yay me.

I guess my days of playing on my Xbox are over now, huh? At least the marathon sessions I've been doing on it since I got the job offer and said sayonara to two-hour commutes, dress shirts, and tight leather shoes. I guess now I need to clock in, participate, actually do some work. It came late, that computer and all its associated stuff. Two days late, which meant all I did was join a meeting or two using my personal cellphone, say a few hellos and thank yous and go back to blasting out the orange pulsating eyes of Mutated Jack, determined to get past that level in Resident Evil Biohazard before putting on my big boy pants and going back to work. But now that was all over. I had to step out of the dilapidated house that served as my refuge in the game and into my office. Mutated Jack is still alive and well.

The laptop is here and cellphone is on its way.

Great.

As I set my laptop up and prepared to call in to support to officially join the company, I become keenly aware of the nothingness around me. No sound. No people. No movement. No nothing. The game was off and I had turned the TV off. There was no sound at all.

Because she's gone.

She hasn't called and neither have I. I'm not planning to. Apparently neither is she. Sick of my shit. Sick of us. Sick of it. That's all she said, at least in a nutshell. Details be damned – who cares if she said it was the way I chew or the smell of my aftershave? None of that gets at the core of it. But I have never been one to delude myself. She's sick of *me*.

Me.

Whatever makes me up; whatever comprises the asshole she walked alongside for 6 years, the parasite sucking at her soul, the leech bleeding her dry. Whatever that is, she's sick of *that*.

And what do you say to that? Really, what do you say when someone tells you that your whole essence pisses them off? That you being you is enough to make them want to vomit, want to rethink their life choices? Do you beg them to give you another chance to try again, to do better, to fix the elusive 'it'? Do you cry? Emasculate yourself in front of her and hope that will make her see you differently? Do you say piss off, good riddance, get thee behind me, Satan, and hold the door open for her to walk out of your life? I don't know. I only know I didn't do any of those things. I just stayed silent, shut my mouth as she picked up her shit and exited stage left... just like the coward she said I am.

Bitch.

Maybe I hate her self-righteous ass a little too.

"*Have you booted up yet? I am prepared to give you the password to access your profile,*" said the guy on the other end whose subcontinent accent told me that it was bright and early the next morning where he was even as it was mid-happy hour for me. I'll never get over how I could be talking to someone damn near a day ahead of me sitting in Maharashtra one minute then call someone three hours behind me in California in the next. That's some back to the future type shit if ever there was.

There it is again... back to the future. Why do I keep making that reference? Do I need to watch that movie again? Need some one-on-one time with Marty McFly?

Note to self: watch *Back to the Future* when you hang up with support. It's important work.

"*Are you there?*"

Persistent little prick, isn't he?

"Yeah, I'm here. I'm still unboxing everything. Hang on a second. I'll make it quick."

I put myself on mute when he started to protest, saying I could call back in to get someone else to help if I needed more time. I don't need more time. I'm almost done.

She used to say I was a wiz at setting up computers back when she was in the mood to say more charitable things. She was right. I can do this with my eyes shut. Normally. This set up – my new set up – should have been done already, unboxed and plugged in. Would have only taken me a minute, as basic as this part is, but I just – I got distracted. Thrown off by the way that the opening of the cardboard cut into the silence so brutally, reminding me. Accusing me.

I am alone.

Utterly fucking alone.

Maybe I should get a dog, I thought, not for the first time in the past few weeks. At least a dog would force me to go outside, out into the fresh air.

My socked feet protested, though, mounting a formidable argument bespeaking comfort, one I couldn't easily topple.

And also...

It's fucking cold outside. Unseasonably cold. That 'I could be talked into putting on the heat' kind of cold, even though summer was barely over and fall hadn't taken a decent hold yet.

So, maybe not now. Maybe when it warms up again, when new leaves sprout and flowers bud.

Maybe when the days are longer and the sun shines brighter.

Maybe she'll come back and love the dog, love the change in me.

Maybe that'll mask the stink she can't bear to smell now.

This isn't even the hard part – just plugging a damned laptop into a socket and letting it charge. Who can't do that? And setting up the monitor... what? Am I confused by all the wires now? The *color-coded* wires? I better get my act together. If I can't set up a simple workstation like this, how am I gonna-

"*Sir, are you there?*" Nondescript South Asian-accented male asked, pulling me out of my reverie.

I look... I am still on mute.

Deep breath.

Off mute.

"Yes, I am. All cabled up. So, what's my password?"

THREE

MSA.
ICA.
TFN.
SSN.
RCA.
ULA.
WTF?

SSN... seriously? When did we start abbreviating social security number? Is it that hard to say the whole thing? When the HR person asked me to confirm it, I almost didn't know what he was referring to. Is 'telephone number' hard to pronounce? Does it get stuck in your mouth?

I s there a college course on navigating corporate America lingo? Acronyms as Language maybe? Or better yet: AAL?

I'm dying.

Listening to people spew out acronym after acronym

through the better than expected speakers on my laptop is fucking killing me. One of the server sets my customer has installed is running an OS that is end of life. That's code for, 'Sorry PMs, you need to tell your customers that they can expect downtime this weekend so we can update the OS. Oh, and that also means I'll need you to be on phone with us too, PMs, to make sure that everything runs smoothly... ok?'

Screw your plans.

Or like Nancy said in *Nightmare on Elm Street*, "Screw your pass."

Screw. Your. Life.

Wait, *end of life*.

Ha, EOL.

FOUR

"I hope we didn't run him off," my new customer said. Her name was Kerry and her voice was chipper. That kind of sound that is meant to be disarming, meant to evoke trust. Positive, nothing can get you down in this big ol' world, happy. But the chuckle that came after the comment – those leading words she hoped would make me say something I hadn't intended to – belied the truth.

"Know what I mean, Chris?"

Yeah I know, alright. I know the last guy quit without notice. Pretty much packed up his laptop, drove it to the closest office, and checked out. Jen, my new manager, didn't want me to know that but people talk. Scoop is always available if you know how to ask the right questions... even if you work from home. A guy in Sales let it spill that my predecessor on this account got fed up with the red tape he always had to jump through to get things done. Said he wanted a job that was meaningful, where he was actually making an impact – whatever that means. The Sales guy, enjoying the sound of his own voice as many of them do, went on to say that the guy was in the middle of a conference call when he decided he'd had enough. The customer – which customer has still not been made clear... maybe Miss Chipper over here? – was asking him about an event that happened the weekend before – an event he had nothing to do with, had only found out about midway through, and had jumped on the support call to try and help troubleshoot on their behalf. The customer was at him, hounding him with questions to no avail. Nothing he replied with was good enough because they were a technical shop - a little savvier than the rest – and everyone knew that. And of course, tech guys don't give two shits about what project managers have to say. The customer was asking him hard questions – the ones that only have 'we can't do that', 'I'll have to look into it', or 'we'll work on it' as answers. Only they wouldn't accept those answers. Of course, they wouldn't. The guy got sick of getting cut off, got sick of hearing the person on the other end of the phone yelling, got sick of his own tech team not interjecting to tell them what really happened and help save his skin – got sick of the whole ball of wax.

"They asked him a question," the Sales guy said, and with an incredulous laugh, he delivered the punchline, "And the guy just said, 'Who gives a shit?' and hung up! He proceeded to log off, unplug his laptop, jump in his car, and leave everything company-related on the executive assistant's desk!"

Classic.

It's the stuff of every PM's nightmares.

Listening to little Miss Chipper prattling on about the account I am taking over, describing their footprint - infrastructure this, test environment that - I wonder if she was the one who pushed him over the edge. Had her happy little voice turned cold mid-sentence? Oh, I know she's capable of it; I can hear the edge it affects at the end of her words, sharp and unyielding. Fake happy.

False.

Call bullshit if you want, apply all the nice little platitudes you want because she sounds like such a 'nice lady', but I've been doing this long enough to know better.

How do I sound to her? Does the cadence of my voice sound inviting, calming, soothing in any way? Maybe. That's what we've been taught – to diffuse situations by any means necessary – so, my voice might have just gone to that subservient place on its own. I've been there before, been that placating, unassuming, 'gonna fix it' guy. Maybe some part of me thinks it'll work this time. But that part of me is a fool if it does.

"Chris?"

Miss Chipper sounded a little off kilter now... and little unhinged. What important, world-changing, mind-blowing thing had she said that I missed? How might she make me pay for it later?

"I'm sure you didn't," I said as if I hadn't been thinking about how she had absolutely, 100% been the reason that Joe or Phil or whatever the dude's name before me was ran for the hills. "You never know what's going on in people's lives."

"True, true," Miss Chipper said, sounding assuaged.

Crisis averted.

"At any rate, I look forward to working with you," I finished, lacing my words with saccharin, hoping they went down smooth.

"Likewise," Miss Chipper's disembodied 'golly gee!' voice cooed in my ear before hanging up.

Bite me.

FIVE

I needed more coffee; that's what finally drove me out of the house.

That was probably a good thing because I was also down to my last pack of ramen.

I should get out anyway, get some sun on my face. It feels like the space is closing in on me. Everything is so... quiet. Silent. The only sound is my voice reverberating off the walls. Unless I turn the TV on, which is rare. For some reason, the tube has been an afterthought recently, giving way to mindless Internet searches about stupid shit like how long a person can survive without drinking water or about that McDonalds hamburger that survived 14 years in some schmuck's pocket. Did he eat it? Maybe not all of it, but I bet he ate some just to see what it tasted like... Time wasters – the TV, the Internet... all of it - but maybe I could try to get into a TV show, occupy my mind with something, give myself something to look forward to. Maybe I would find out what was going on now on *Power* or start the *Jack Ryan* series.

Maybe.

I can almost hear her saying that *Power* did it just as well as *Dallas* did – maybe better. I can see her face contorting when she talked about the possible motives, going deep into the storylines almost as if Ghost was her second cousin and she had babysat Tariq and Raina when they were little. I always went there when I thought about that show, any show, anything connected to the life I lived before. Her. The smile that crept onto my lips when I fell too deep made me angry, sick to my stomach, nostalgic, sad as hell.

Some fresh air will definitely do me good.

I checked my schedule to make sure I didn't have another orientation or customer transition in the next hour. That's been my daily schedule since I started: meet with this one to learn about internal tools, meet with that one to learn about product lines, then meet with another one to discuss transitioning accounts. Repeat. Lots of systems, lots of products, lots of disjointed processes, and passwords. So many passwords... The minutia of corporate America. I hear there will be meetings to summarize these meetings, meetings to talk about scheduling new meetings, then meetings to discuss processes that are nice to haves but are never gonna happen unless they occur in future meetings. And, sadly, that all makes sense to me. It's the world I know. They're all the same, these mid-level IT shops. Whether they service larger customers with more money than they can shake a stick at or mom and pops with just enough to cover basic backup, every company hocks product the same way. It's like putting lipstick on a pig when you get right down to it.

I stand up only to feel like I'm learning how to do it all over again. I look at the time and see that it's already well past noon. The last time I looked at the clock, it was 8:20 a.m. Half the day is gone and I had no idea. It was disconcerting, to say the least. Losing time like that, missing days, events, etc. because you're sitting at your desk the whole time, it's... it takes a little getting used to. Working from *home* takes some getting used to. There's no downtime, no disconnection. Sure, it could be about getting laundry done, watching daytime tv, and lounging in pajamas all day if you wanted it to be, but then you'd be looking for a job in short order. No, working from home is a different animal than I ever expected going in – probably different than anyone ever thought it would be when they were presented with the idea. They expect you to be available... all... the... time. Because what else are you doing? If you weren't at your desk, you might be playing video games, sleeping, picking your navel in the warmth of the sun – whatever, right? It's easy to assume someone was fucking around when you can't reach them, so working from home is as much an effort in remaining present as it is being a competent self-starter worthy of the flexibility the opportunity affords. Add in being a 24/7 resource and you're a goner. Want to call me at 7:45 pm when I should be parked in front of my TV watching *Jeopardy*? Sure, no problem, I'll just rewind it. Want me to log in and run a diagnostic report for you at 2:3fuck in the morning because a customer's circuit is flapping? Can do – sleep's overrated anyway.

I haven't been outside in days... at least I don't think I have.

And I just *got* this damned job...

———

T he sun is bright.
   Not movie bright, that artificial, 'so blinding, I can't see anything' bright, but still bright. There was no shielding of eyes, squinting, kvetching of any kind (nothing to see here, folks), not really. But it was like the noonday sun

was shining right on my head kind of bright. Almost like a spotlight.

I drove to the supermarket feeling out of sorts. How long had it really been since I'd gone out to get food? I don't eat a lot. I can exist on ramen noodles and crackers for days if I wanted to. And I had, hadn't I? Just sat there eating reconstituted food with salty broth and crumbly crackers. Just because I could. Might have been a decent weight loss strategy; my pants are sitting low on my hips now; they're much looser than I remember them being. There's that.

As I walked into the store, my little basket in hand, the question of pants comes to mind again. I look down and catch of glimpse of what I labeled pants in my mind but were really pajamas. Old pajamas, in fact. Ones that I was suddenly sure, without a modicum of doubt, had a gaping hole in them.

While I stood in the brightly lit supermarket – what is with all the 'bright light, bright light' commentary? Who am I, Gizmo? But seriously, are those, LED lightbulbs? Jesus. – I was assaulted by all sorts of questions that I should have given some thought to while I was still within the confines of my own home and could do something about them:

Had I combed my hair?

When was the last time I *washed* my hair?

When was the last time I took a shower or brushed my teeth? The effects of halitosis aren't much of a problem these days with no one to kiss or pull away from me when they caught a whiff, so I really don't know.

That fact that I don't know the answer to any of those questions startled me. That I hadn't even hazarded a glance at myself before coming outside and being in the public is a little disconcerting too, if I'm being honest. When had I slipped into this headspace – the one where I don't care about what I look like or what I'm wearing because I don't plan on interacting with anyone anyway? Why was it so easy to stop giving a damn? Because I don't – that much is true. I could give two shits anymore about what people thought of me and my bedhead and my mismatched clothes. Why would I? I don't know anyone here – we moved to a neighborhood three towns away from where our apartments had been... where we still liked each other. I didn't know anyone and no one knew me and that was just fine, I thought, as I picked at some dried crud on my shirt. But still, maybe a little less disheveled and a little more, I don't know, washed would be better, hmm? Maybe next time I'll take a washcloth to my face and my underarms. Give the world a little less 'here he is, folks, in all his glory: Exhibit A: Joe Schmo, telecommuter.'

An old lady shoves past me, her house dress billowing around pasty, frail legs that still managed to move her along at a pretty good clip. She eyed me from under a barely contained salt and pepper crown of hair, milky eyes tired but focused. She didn't have to look over her shoulder at me, her face reflecting disdain, a frown mingling with the deep wrinkles that cut rivers and roads on her sagging cheeks, but she did.

She saw something she didn't like.

I was tempted to return the look, show her that I could muster up a snarl for a stranger too if I really wanted to, but I caught hold of myself in time. I might be a little out of sorts, might be operating a little to the left of my usual, but I haven't lost *all* of my manners... at least not yet.

What must I look like if little old grandmas were making faces at me in the doorway of a supermarket?

I had stopped walking as I contemplated my life, I realized. Maybe that's why the woman gave me the side eye. Maybe it was everything.

Maybe she was right.

With a sigh, I moved further into the store.

It's like an alternate reality in here.

People trudging around, aimlessly turning into aisles, eying the contents of shelves listlessly. Slow, dim-witted people moving from side to side with the unsteady gait of the infirm – the truly old or sick who have to lean on their canes to take even the smallest step.

Midday at the supermarket.

It was like *Night of the Living Dead* in here, I thought without hesitation, so like zombies the shoppers, cashiers, and even the pharmacist seemed, with their sallow skin and lackluster eyes. *Night of the Living Dead*, yeah. Zombies, but those specifically, their white clothes glowing against the dark of night. Not like *The Walking Dead*. The zombies in the supermarket moved way too slow for that comparison to stick.

Zoned out.

Catatonic.

I can only imagine what the microexpressions flitting across my face must have looked like to anyone aware enough to notice. Most of them showed some variant of disgust, likely.

Probably.

Cheddar cheese.

Swiss cheese.

Pacing bodies swaying indiscriminately in the aisles.

Block.

Shredded.

A woman, lost in her own head, gray dotting her temples, glasses perched on her nose ambled over. Then she's standing next to me, staring at the cheese like she doesn't know which one to get.

Finely shredded.

Shredded – as in plain old cut into strips, shredded.

The corner of her eye twitches – actually shudders, like wind causing the surface of standing water to ripple... like a shiver from a cold breeze.

Made with 2% or whole milk.

Come on, I urge silently from my place in front of the canned pastry tubes – the ones you need to bang on the side of your counter to make the dough explode inside them... the ones that could put your eye out if you weren't careful - *come on*, I press with my eyes, if not my voice, *live a little*.

Her eyes cascade down the packages of processed gunk – that weird spray cheese, those perfect American cheese squares wrapped in plastic. She tripped over the bleu cheese, the goat cheese, the queso fresco, seeing but not seeing, recognizing but not caring. Oh yes, she knows I'm watching her. She sees me from the corner of her eye even as it twitch – twitch – twitches.

She licks her lips when I shift from the balls of my feet to the heel. Balls to heels. Back and forth. Back...

Cottage cheese.

Cream cheese.

How about goat cheese, hmm? Creamy and white. Soft, like a cotton ball against a splintering table. Soft, unlike its overripe sister, brie. Soft like waiting skin in the warmth of the noonday sun.

Soft.

Supple.

Pliant.

Ricotta cheese.

Her lips part to reveal the bottoms of a blackened upper row of teeth; ridged, the mamelons unsmoothed, unnaturally prominent.

Jagged enough to cut her own flesh.

In fact, I was sure she had cut her tongue, her finger, and

anything else that had come into contact with those teeth many a time. And just as I knew that was fact, I knew that she liked it too.

Colby cheese.

Monterey Jack.

Muenster.

She snickered... and bit her bottom lip.

A trickle of blood blossomed against it, rising like a fount, spreading, bubbling over.

Red.

Bright.

Dark.

Dead.

I knew it.

I need cheese.

Suddenly I need cheese more than I've ever needed anything before.

What do *I* want today? What's my fancy? Maybe a mix like Jalapeño Jack for my spicy burger or that gimmicky Mexican blend, which is just a mix of some regular old cheese bagged together with the illusory "quesadilla" cheese (yeah, I see you). Or maybe I need some old-fashioned mold in the form of Neufchâtel or maybe the saucy 'not cheese', Velveeta, for the nachos I didn't know I wanted.

My mouth is open and I don't know why.

She can hear me breathing.

A smile plays at the corner of her lips as she looks at me – looks right at me – without ever turning her head.

Just one beady little eye.

Parmesan.

Asiago.

I reach out to grab something, anything.

I beat her to it, her taloned hand jutting out a fraction of a second after mine to land on the thin skin that covered the bones on the back of my hand... metacarpal bones, fragile bones like those of a baby's, every detail exposed under the skin, protruding like a skeleton's – brittle, flimsy: weak.

A fraction of a second.

Long enough for me to wonder if I would ever get to taste the fresh mozzarella my hand had landed on, little balls of the stuff wet in the package, moving around like eyeballs in a sensory bowl – long enough for me to wish I hadn't reached for it at all...

Eggs.

Eyeballs in a sensory bowl are usually made of boiled eggs.

Eggs.

Brown.

Farm raised.

Quail eg-

What the hell?

Where had that come from? Where had that weird vision that felt so much like a part of my mind, felt so inherently in place that I am not sure it hadn't always been there, even now as I try to shake it away... Where had that *come* from? That second when the eggs weren't eggs... not from any bird I've ever seen before, anyway... when the whites were made of blood instead of that gelatinous goop... when... when had those thoughts taken up residence in my mind, waiting for the chance to show themselves?

Balut.

It's gotta be that.

I fucking knew watching that show about crazy things that people eat was a wrong turn. I thought it would be the spiders that would come back to haunt me, was sure that dreams of tarantula legs playing footsie with my tonsils as I tried swallow them down were in my future, without a doubt. Not quite dead, these. Better take it up with that dude selling them by the dozen at his booth in the Skuon market square. But no, it was that little baby duck that some people have no qualms about eating whole, its little bones soft enough to swallow down at 18 or 19 days old, that came back to bite me in the ass.

Here, in the middle of the supermarket. Next to the cheese lady.

Garbage bags, bread, apple pie, and now, apparently cheese in my cart. A nice bag of shredded sharp cheddar for the folks that were too lazy to get a block and shred it themselves. And mozzarella balls – can't forget those.

Baby birds with blind eyes and spider legs instead of wings in my head.

Great.

Welcome, nightmare. Your table for one is ready.

SIX

"We might have to roll back the change. Let's call the systems architect to have them weigh in, because they should know if —"

I had hoped I would like this job.

Really, I did.

I need to like something in my life right now – my empty, marginal existence. But after multiple service events brought on by fat-fingered code, night after night of emergency calls, people bumping into cables and dislodging them, and hotfixes that were more like hot messes, I don't think I do. In fact, as I sit here at 3:00 a.m. on a Sunday morning, yet again, listening to dead silence before the rousing of another poor soul out of their slumber is suggested, I know damned well I don't. Right now it's silent - the kind of silence that makes you think you might be able to go off and do something else while they sort it out, the kind that lets you confidently stand up, unplug the laptop, and go into the family room to watch a movie while they plod through, only to have your name called out of nowhere, the voice saying it booming through

27

the speakers, definitively popping your bubble. It's almost like they know you've moved away from your desk, somehow jimmied the ankle monitor or the tether the binds you to the chair leg to, I don't know, grab a cup of coffee, stretch before your spine compresses, rendering you useless in your old age, or, horror of horrors, go to the bathroom. They know. Somehow, they know. They must, because it's in that moment, that perfect time when you've stepped away far enough to create a pause in answering when your name is called, thus outing the fact that you are not sitting in front of your laptop after all - it's in that moment that they speak your name.

What's the customer's temperature?

Can you test things from your side?

Is there anything in their environment that you can identify that might have caused this?

Chris??

The answer is invariably 'no' by default. Not because you can't answer the question or contribute meaningfully to the conversation, but because you didn't *hear* the question, not completely. Because you were standing in the hallway contemplating the color of your wall when the person on the other line starts asking. You try to repeat the snippet of what you heard them saying in your head as quickly as you can, hoping you can puzzle together what they were asking enough to hazard a guess at the answer, but you can't. No one can – that never works. And while its ok when the executives say things like, "I'm sorry mate, I was multitasking. Can you repeat that?' or 'I didn't catch that – what are you asking?', both of which are code for 'I am not paying attention to this bullshit, so say it again', no one ever takes kindly when a lowly minion does that. That's the plight of the individual contributor - the manager who only manages customers, not people. The guy at the bottom of shitball hill. Instead of showing how busy you are, asking for someone to repeat themselves is like shining the red laser of an assassin's gun on your forehead. Repeat? Why? You weren't paying attention? Why? Because you have something better to do?

Yes, actually. Fuck yes. How about sleeping? How about eating? How about anything other than sitting here listening to silence, afraid to move because your name might be called from somewhere out of the ether?

"What internal IPs did they use?"

Her voice jolted me out of my daydream. I'm standing in my living room, a room I might have gone into the least out of every room in the house despite it being right across the hall from my office. There's no furniture in it, and only one lamp: a standing halogen-looking thing that actually takes a regular bulb rather than that circular contraption that used to burn too hot and zap all the bugs in the house. There are black things in the bottom of the decorative frosted light shell, though. A sea of black things – big black things - haphazardly lying about, one on the other, piled on top of each other like garbage at the dump. What are those... stink bugs? Beetles? One of those shadowed things is moving, crawling up the side, trying to get out, using the other dark things – the bodies - as leverage.

"Can you confirm the IPs, please?"

Me?

Of course she's talking to me.

Out of all the other people on the conference bridge doing nothing – you could even hear one dude snoring before the host muted his line – out of all of those people, of *course* she was talking to me.

And I'm staring at a bug graveyard in my light fixture.

Quick! What the hell is she asking?

"You need the IPs for..."

Does that also sound like, 'I wasn't listening – please repeat yourself'?

Probably, but whatever.

The living room is so empty. Like the rest of the house. The house is so empty. So very empty. There's literally nothing in here but me, the bed, the TV, and some boxes that I don't have the compulsion to unpack. I don't want to unpack because I don't want to stay long. I shouldn't stay here – it's nothing but a money pit for me now, not the memory maker I thought it would be.

Not the memory maker I had *hoped* it would be.

I need space...

She had said that twice; once when she wanted space for her art studio, needing more room to lay out her easels, paints, all the stuff she used to make her own canvases, because somehow that spoke to her authentic self, she said, and then she said it once again when she was walking out the door. Space. That's all I have now is space. This big house, my days and nights – they're chock full of it.

"For the ser-"

"Ok, gotcha," I said, cutting her off. Because I knew what she needed now... it was the same thing I gave her an hour ago. But ok, I can give it to her... again.

IPs sent.

Quiet again.

Quiet always.

SEVEN

I don't know what I expected. Would my front door be wide open, the entryway looking like a gaping maw with ragged teeth and a discolored tongue? Would people be looking inside, peering, trying to see what was lurking in the shadows? Would there be debris left behind, scraps of paper, paper cups and plastic cutlery, the minutia of life collected on my stoop like tumbleweed? There was none of that. And that was infinitely worse.

How did she know I was out? I couldn't help but wonder. She hadn't knocked on the door one day when I was sitting in my office on one of my many (many) conference calls. She didn't walk up to the door, see me in the window, and turn back – I would have noticed her before she saw me. I'm always looking outside while I listen to people argue, posture, and prattle. Always looking for something, anything: her.

I park my car in the garage, so she couldn't tell if I was home or not just by driving by.

There's no landline to call and breathe heavily on.

So, how did she know?

The day she did it, I had done something so unlike me, too. Something I had talked about doing, had always said would be nice to do if I ever moved to the suburbs, but never envisioned myself actually doing for real. At least, not alone. But there I was, taking a freaking walk, of all things. Getting some sun on my face and some fresh air through my hair. I had even dressed for it, threw on some shorts and a t-shirt that only had a few holes, and those were hidden – in the pits, mostly. I didn't shower, though – there was no need for that... all I was going to do was get sweaty again anyway, so why go through the effort?

I was gone for 30 minutes, 45 max. How did she manage to get in, grab all her stuff, and leave without a trace?

She was gone.

And so was everything that reminded me of her.

There were no brake lights ducking around the corner as I walked up to the house, no perfume sweetening the stale air in the foyer.

Nothing.

How did she know when to come; when to sneak in and grab her shit? Had she put some GPS tracking app on my phone so she knew when the bear finally came out of the cave? Was she old school watching the house from her car like one of those TV detectives from the 70s? Unlikely. Knowing her, she probably knocked on the door, found the house empty and used her key to get in. It can hardly be considered sneaking when you use a key to get into your own house, whether or not you claimed it as such anymore.

So, that's it, then? That's the whole ball of wax? We're really not going to talk about it? Curse at each other? Throw shit around? It's just... over?

I don't know how to feel about that. Actually, I don't know how to feel about anything anymore.

My phone rings in my back pocket. The sound echoes off the unadorned walls and empty rooms. My computer rings too, adding its chime to the mix, creating a deafening cacophony of real and reverberated sound.

Unmelodious and shrill.

Mechanical and monotone.

Battling.

Warring.

Insistent.

Persistent.

Blocking out all else.

Both devices going off at the same time can only mean one thing. Work beckons.

Fuck.

EIGHT

"**H**ey!" The doorbell surprised me – literally made me jump out of my skin. I was watching a YouTube video about William Perry, aka The Fridge from the Chicago Bears, when the chime pulled me back to reality. I got up from my desk before I was ready, feeling a little lightheaded and wobbly. Have I eaten today? No, of course not. That would be too much like what normal people did... too much like right. Did I eat last night? I don't know.

I flung the door open a little faster than I meant to, a strange eagerness to see who was outside, to actually *see* the outside taking over me. As I felt the air on my face I realized I hadn't had that sensation in a long time. The last time I had there were some kids asking for money for their team to go on an end of season trip. Sweaty and tired – they said they had been at it all day and I was their last house – they delivered their speech and I had to give it to them, it was compelling. I gave them some money, even spared them the advice sitting on the tip of my tongue, that bitter old man armchair wisdom that screamed, 'Stop panhandling and get a job!' from inside my not yet middle-aged body. The next time the doorbell rang and two young men dressed in identical slacks, dress shirts, and ties, one holding what could have been a bible and the other some kind of pamphlet – Mormon? Jehovah's Witness? Some sect with a commune on a remote farm in the hills? – came calling, I didn't answer.

I took a deep breath of it; the air smelled, I don't know... fresh? Better than whatever I was breathing in day in and day out in my pent-up house.

It was the UPS guy.

He was standing there holding what looked like an old label maker, typing something in with one finger. How can people really hunt and peck anymore? With the advent of smartphones, how could someone really not understand how to engage their thumbs and be under 65 years old? I stared at him, marveling at this dinosaur, this throwback to times past, when people had flip phones and scroll wheels... and yet, is that a Bluetooth earpiece I see in his ear?

"Hey, yeah," I said, hoping that maybe he didn't hear my surprised yell from inside the house, but knowing he probably had. The eagerness in my voice wasn't lost on me.

The UPS guy looked up with a non-committal smile that was aimed somewhere behind me – it was so obvious that he wasn't looking at me, I almost turned around to see what was drawing his attention.

"Sign right here," he said and diverted his eyes while simultaneously shoving the device he's holding at me.

"Yeah, sure, of course," I stuttered, not knowing why.

"Nice day out today, right?" I said, hoping it sounds like absentminded chatter and not the highlight of my existence right now.

"Yeah, I guess," he responded, never looking up, disinterested, ready to go.

"Yeah, I haven't been out yet, but today does seem like a nice one."

And? What made me prattle on about shit he didn't care about? Why did I feel the need to justify myself, explain the way I look – mismatched pajama bottoms and top, slippers with a hole in them... hell, my pajama pants almost certainly have a hole in them too. My hair is likely sticking up, my face probably has lines on it from when I had fallen asleep at my desk with my head in my arms a little while ago – why did I feel the need to lie that away? Make the lines be there because I had just woken up after a night on the town, or because I had just come back late from overseas, or something... anything except the pathetic reality that I fell asleep at my desk because I have no life and I am fucking always at my desk. He never even looked at me, didn't give a shit what I looked like. He had a job to do: give me my box and then move on the next. Nothing more, nothing less.

"Yeeeeup," he said, compliantly as is the UPS way. It won't do to piss of the customers, no siree.

I sniffed, feigning disinterest.

He looked at the molding above my front door.

Get the fuck out of here, then. If you can't spare a word to a stranger during your "busy" day, go on back to whatever else you have in your life. Drive that truck back to the warehouse and clock out. Get in your not old enough to be considered a classic sportscar and pick up your small-town pretty girlfriend, the one who'll give it up to you as long as you promise to take her away from this shithole someday, go tell her-

He nodded at me, his eyes trained below my waist.

What the fuck?

Hey look, buddy, I don't know what you think I meant,

but it wasn't that. I am not interested in –

"You, ah, finished sir?" he said and looked below my waist again, at the hand that was holding the signature pad hostage.

I laughed a little too loud for a little too long as I fumbled, trying to hand him the device and not drop my box at the same time. He took it in stride and flashed another disinterested smile as he backed away from my door and headed down the walk toward the UPS truck. I waved at him as he drove down the street, watching as he rounded the curve and headed to his next drop. He didn't wave back.

I looked out at the houses across from mine, each of them shuttered and closed off in the middle of the day. People that work in offices or stores or at gas stations or strip clubs live there. People who actually get out of the house and talk to other people occupy those rooms and walk those hallways.

I turned back to look into my house. It was quiet and gray inside, the sunlight cutting a wedge on the floor in the foyer, not quite making it into the main hall.

Dark.

Quiet.

Still.

Shadows layered upon shadows in the dining room – dark like night. What's in there? I never go in that room, never go on that side of the house, really. It's the "entertaining" side – the one with the formal living room and a dining room that could house a 10-seater table. That's the side of the house she had been most excited about. Said she couldn't wait to decorate it for Christmas with poinsettias and gold chargers and whatever else she went on about. I don't go in there. I only use the office, the kitchen, the bedroom, and the bathroom... still.

Had she set up her grandmother's curio in the dining room before she left? She had been going on and on about wanting to do it. Said she wanted to give it a proper home. She must have done just that, and in short order, though I can't imagine her pushing it into place. She was always afraid to touch it, afraid to break one of the glass doors or loosen the crystal knobs. Precious cargo, she called it, and I knew better than to challenge her about that. Even so, that must be what I see up against the wall, the denser shadow against a lighter one. It looks solid, distinct, tangible.

Wouldn't she have taken it? Wouldn't that have been one of the first things to get moved out of the house when she left? She would never leave the curio here with me. What if I broke it? What if I ruined it the way she always feared I would by bumping into it, or leaning against it, or just looking at it too hard? Wouldn't she be afraid that I would break the damned thing just to get back at her? Throw a shoe into it and watch the glass doors splinter into tiny little shards all over the carpet? No, she wouldn't worry about that. I'm not a spiteful person, at least not normally. Even-keeled, level-headed, passive even, if you went by her description of me in the last few months of our relationship. Never spiteful. But fucking up that piece of knock off, dime-store furniture masquerading as an art deco antique is sounding real good right about now.

Dark.

Too dark.

Light should be glinting off the glass and the silver braces if the curio was really back there in the corner, even if just a little bit of light hit it.

Leaning... listing...?

Shit.

If that damned thing falls and breaks for real, she'll blame me... she'll never forgive me.

Shifting...?

The slam of the door nearly made my heart stop in my chest.

Breathing fast.

Chest heaving.

My breath was rank under my nose.

I'm inside.

All the way inside.

When the hell had I walked inside?

When the hell had I taken steps into the house, steps toward the dining room, toward the leaning, listing curio that couldn't be here, shouldn't be here...?

Why had I slammed the door?

I realized with painful clarity that I was still staring at the corner where the curio – it *is* the curio, right? It has to be the curio... right? – stood, watching the darkness play around the edges, seeming to writhe around them, cascading over them like billowing smoke. Moving. That bitch is moving. Undulating, rippling -

How did I slam the door?

Two, no, three steps into the house... how did I slam the door? How had I managed to still have my hand on the door-knob from that distance?

That nagging thought tickles the nape of my neck, trying to coax my head to turn around and take a look, but I don't want to. I am afraid to look away from the curio in the corner, the thing that is too damned short to be her curio, beast that it was. That monstrosity stood almost as tall as me but the shadow cast by whatever was in the corner seemed to be several inches shorter... short... like her. I was afraid to turn away because the curio – that thing – was moving. It was moving, rolling its hips and shoulders in the shadows, and I was rapt, watching its body rock and sway as the darkness came off it like mist.

The phone rang.

I dropped my box. Like a scared little kid, I dropped my box of what was probably company gear (more tchotchkes and logo-laden backpacks – yay me!). I bent to pick it up out of pure muscle memory but froze when I realized I had taken my eyes off the thing in the corner, the thing that was moving, the thing that was *coming*.

I shifted my eyes slowly, terrified that it was there, that it had cleared the space between me and the dining room in that instant and was there, ready to reveal what it truly was.

The ringing sounded like it was coming from another dimension.

A car rumbled by, its windows catching the sun and throwing it into my house whose closed curtains and shut blinds were reluctant to receive it. My desk was illuminated as were the stains and dried drops of food. The foyer was lit up, showing just how barren it truly was. The living room and dining room walls caught a ray or two, revealing their emptiness – no pictures up yet, folks. Maybe never. The car passed by the house moving the sunlight first through and then out of it. Fast, the return to darkness. It sent a shiver down my spine. I looked in the corner again, screwing on my courage before the light disappeared altogether. There was no curio. There was no "thing". There was nothing.

Ringing... again.

Shrill and contemptuous.

Seemed to fill my head, the foyer, the whole house.

Sigh.

I'm gonna open the blinds, I resolve, as I head back into the office. *Gonna brighten the place up a bit.*

I nod to myself as I pick up the phone, even as the hairs on the back of my neck stand on end.

NINE

She killed him.

     She did it because he wouldn't stop mowing a stripe into her yard.

I saw them standing on their respective lawns, hands on their hips, frowning, glaring, rolling their eyes again. It was the second time this month, probably the tenth time since I've moved in. Sometimes I heard them shouting at each other, sarcasm dripping from every word. Other times there was a tension outside that I couldn't place, something pulling me to come closer to the window, to open the blinds, to rubberneck at the accident across the street that surely awaited my greedy eyes. It was those times when I watched from my window to see them leaning into each other menacingly, promising more to come if the other didn't shut their trap, fix their problem – give in – that I could do what everyone else was doing: watch them like they were a reality TV show.

With my presence obstructed from view by the glare of the sun, I could do what everyone else was doing... eavesdrop, form an opinion about something that had nothing to do with

me: be nosy. I couldn't wait to see what would happen next –
would she haul off and slap him one day? Would he puff out
his chest and try to intimidate her back to her own front door?
Would they yell and scream so loud that one of the other
neighbors, civic-minded lot that they were, called the police?
The idea of one of those scenarios coming to life was so good
I almost popped popcorn and pulled up a chair. Every...
single... time. Whatever was going to happen across the
street, I'm here for it.

And so I find myself this Saturday morning in raggedy
pajama bottoms and a smelly t-shirt unabashedly watching
the scene play out on the lawn across the street. I make no
attempt to hide the fact that I'm watching: I almost opened
the door so I would have an unobstructed view. Because
something went down over there. The dam had finally
broken.

There was an ambulance parked in front of the house.
Two police cars too. Parked in front of *his* house.

Pete had finally pushed Carla too far.

What's the protocol? What are you supposed to do when
one of your neighbors gets carted off in an ambulance, feet
first and bagged? Is it ok to go outside and stand guard, form a
processional line to send him off? Are you supposed to meet
each other in the street and clasp hands, hug shoulders, heads
swiveling on necks while you talk over each other in your zeal
to discuss what happened, comment on how good a man he
was, all the while gawking, peering, hoping for a glimpse of
the body?

Because everyone wants to see what he looks like, right?

Everyone wants to know if his end was bloody, if his face
was contorted in pain, frozen that way for the embalmer to
fix. Everyone wants to know what she did to take him down,
marathon-running, health food junkie that he was.

Was it poison? Right in his whey protein shake, just a little bit of poison... by the time you taste the bitter, it's too late.

Or was it a knife in the neck? Maybe he came at her, mad about the way she talked to him, maybe he tripped and fell and she saw her chance and took it, maybe he was drunk and angry but sloppy and careless and she was sober as a stone and plunged the knife deep.

Maybe they were having an affair and all of that arguing about the lawn was really about something else – something deeper.

Like, 'Why don't you ever stay the night?'

'You know I can't. I have a family.'

And, 'What do I mean to you? Am I just a quick fuck when you want to do something freaky?'

'Don't fuck this up for us! Why are you making a scene?'

And then she says, 'You like it when I make a scene, don't you, Daddy? That's why you keep fucking up my lawn, so I'll come out here and get you going, huh?'

And he's all, 'That's right baby, you know I do. Why don't you slap me, huh? Why don't you slap me right now where everyone can see? Slap me hard enough that it'll leave a mark for me to look at in the mirror tomorrow.'

Is it ok to stand in a crowd of people who you call neighbors and act like that means something – something like family – when it really doesn't... when neighbors are really just people who liked the same kind of house as you – people whom you don't really know, couldn't list a single thing about other than their first and maybe last names... is it ok to stand among these folks and ogle, gawk, stare unabashedly into the open mouth of Pete's door, writhing in anticipation under the guise of disbelief, if anyone even bothered with pretense, that is?

Maybe.

But why would you when you could watch the show from inside? You could pick out the players without being seen, put the pieces together without all the chatter.

Alone.

No one will look at me funny for having my door open while I watch the spectacle in front of me. They would just assume I was the queasy type, that I couldn't take the idea of, gasp, a neighbor being carted away dead. They would think me sensitive, introspective, hell, that might work in my favor. Maybe the perky runner down the street would notice that I didn't – couldn't? – come out and feel sorry for me. Pete, the newly deceased, did live right across the street from me - maybe he and I were close; no one could say for sure either way, right? Maybe he and I drank beers in our backyards in the evenings and shot the shit about politics and sports and whatever other surface crap people talked about when they didn't have anything in common other than their addresses. Maybe, just maybe she would see me standing there uncomfortable in my doorway (Note to self: shift my weight on my feet a little. Make it look good.), face blank, eyes unreadable and decide that she needed to help me through it. That no one else but her could help me heal. Maybe she'd bring me a meal, eat it with me, crack open a bottle of wine, fall into my bed, fuck my brains out.

Yeah, I'll stay right here.

Cue the fidgeting in the doorway.

The red color splash of the ambulance gave the neighborhood – its grass, houses, even people – a desaturated, monochrome appearance. That it was an overcast morning didn't help matters and maybe that was good. Bright sunlight, a happy blue sky, and kids on bikes along the periphery wouldn't do when a gurney was being wheeled out of a house, the telltale black body bag perched on top of it. Everything was appropriately solemn. Mother Nature sure knows how to set a scene right.

And then, finally, some action.

The EMS tech came to the door, leaving the house backwards as he descended the first step. This was the spot where Pete loved to launch his rebuttal from, never starting the argument, but happy to oblige it, yelling and pointing and nudging back his dog, some little yapper of a thing, from trying to get outside to see what was going on. The gurney followed, covered with a body bag, as expected. Formless, but still one could see that there was something disproportionate about the top. It wasn't flat, the body bag, it wasn't even. The hands probably did it, I figured, my extensive knowledge of the dealings of death coming to the fore – thank you SVU and CSI. Hands clasped over the stomach, just like they would be in his coffin.

I wonder what my face looked like when Pete came to the door. Shaky hand on his temple, the other arm pressed around his waist to hug himself, Pete leaned against the door for support as the EMS team took the body out... whose body, though? I was so sure it was him, confident that either his lover or his wife had finished him off, that I had never even considered an alternative. My mind raced as it sorted through scenarios – maybe it's the wife, angry after finding out that his antagonistic relationship with the neighbor was just a ruse to hide their steamy passion. Did she come at him with accusations spewing from her lips, cursing, yelling, challenging?

Did she tell him to get out – to get the fuck out! – and that he would be hearing from her lawyer?

Did she strike out at him, try to slap him and that's when he lost control – hitting, throwing, shaking her until she was close to unconsciousness? Did he tell her he hated her? That he wished he'd never married her?

Did he tell her how much of a better fuck the neighbor lady was? That he loved the way she sucked his dick – could suck it so well and make him come in minutes whereas she had never been able to do so at all, had always been more worried about how she looked doing it, how long it was taking to finish the whole thing?

Did he tell her how much he loved to pull the neighbor lady's hair - what was her name, anyway? - and how much she loved it too, how she begged for it, cried for it?

Did he pull his wife's hair then, showing her what it felt like to be treated that way, ask her if she liked it?

Did she tell him he was a monster?

Did he ruin her then or was there more?

My mouth hung open; I could feel the air dipping in and out, sampling the inside of it. How many people saw me standing there like that, stunned, shocked? How many people wondered why?

The perky runner down the street was there, wading through the crowd, her running path disturbed by the morning's events. She stopped to talk to the nosy old lady who lived on the other side of the street from where he stood, just a few doors down from the supposed dead man who was, at this moment, very much alive. She was likely asking what happened, that would be the normal question under those circumstances. It's not every day you go out for a run only to come back to your street to find an ambulance in front of your neighbor's house and most of the residents outside in their pajamas. And the old lady was the right person to ask because if anyone knew what was going on, it was her. The woman sat in her window and kept watch over the street all day long. I wouldn't be surprised if she sat on a crapper in her chair, had a mini fridge on the floor next to her and a microwave within arm's reach, all so she didn't have to leave her perch, not even for a second. There would be no porch piracy happening on her watch, no siree. No rambunctious kids knocking over mailboxes. Not here. Not while the sheriff was in town. I've seen her sleeping in that chair like it was her bed – not the 'oops, I fell asleep in my chair' kind of rest, but the 'it's time to turn in for the night' type of slumber; purposeful and deliberate. Yeah, if anyone would know what happened, she would.

They spoke standing close to each other, lips unavailable for him to read. Head shakes and nods. Pained expressions. A palm to the chest. And then the neighborhood guard dog turned her head to regard something else, moving ever so slowly as she wrenched her eyes away from the flashing lights, the nervous chatter, the prying eyes to fix them on the houses across the street, empty for the most part, all its inhabitants having funneled out into the lane to gather with their neighbors in the face of such an unfortunate event. All but one.

I didn't see the perky runner's head turn toward me too because I was too busy closing the door. I didn't need to see it, though. I knew what I would find in those eyes.

Did she think maybe I did it? Had the old cow maybe told her that she sees me looking out of the window sometimes, looking at people as they walk by? Watching, wanting, coveting? Did she tell her that I sometimes trained my eyes on her, looking long after she had passed my door to catch a glimpse of her form, firm legs, the jiggle in her ass as she ran? Did she say that I didn't answer the door when she came by carrying a malformed quick bread that was supposed to scream, 'Welcome to the neighborhood!' but instead held up the sign of the cross and said, 'Beware!'? Probably. And it was all true. But that didn't mean I did anything. That didn't mean I got tired of all the yelling across the street and went over there to shut someone's mouth myself, wielding a knife at the first warm body I saw because I was sick of it, so sick of all the fucking noise. That didn't mean I went in there to show the man just what I thought of his granola-eating self-righteous ass and sunk my knife into whoever answered the door without looking and missed, dear God I missed him and hit his wife instead. His innocent wife with the most beautiful cleavage I've ever seen through the sliver of curtain that I hid behind to spy on people. It didn't mean any of that.

And what about her?

She watched people out of her window just as much as I did. I have spent time watching her watching people, so I know. Maybe she got up one day and did something about all the yelling, hmm? Maybe she's the one who walked in the house, guns blazing, and shot, just shot without looking, shot without thinking and hit the wrong person. Maybe it isn't the wife who's dead. Fuck, I don't even *know* who's dead... Maybe it's one of the kids...

The ambulance pulls away but I can't look now, not with that old cow standing outside staring at my house, making the perky runner and the carpenter next door and the tech writer from across the street who goes out even less than I do look at my door. I can't look now with the body bag laying on my porch waiting, a gift ready to be unwrapped.

TEN

I t's dark.
So dark.

Conference calls in the middle of the night or, I guess it's technically the wee hours of the morning- whenever the fuck this is – they don't get any easier the more you do them. I should know. I've been on more than my share.

Voices pierce the darkness. The small light on my desk only emits a cone of muted yellow, tentative as it cuts through the blackness to light the papers strewn atop the surface. It seems hesitant, this light, afraid... almost like it feels the darkness could swallow it up, sop it up entirely like bread does gravy. And then it would be gone, gone, gone.

Gone.

She is gone.

Definitely gone.

Like the not coming back kind of gone that feels hollow, numb around the edges instead of solid or stinging. She's gone and I'm here, this big house swallowing me up, smothering me with its heavy air and inky black shadows. Gone like she was never actually here at all. I would believe that if I could, would cling to it if it would fill the emptiness I felt, but I knew it wouldn't. Because she is gone.

Definitely, without a doubt gone.

Maybe she has someone else. It's been months now – maybe she found someone else at a happy hour or the gym or wherever she spends her time these days. Maybe she swiped right on some hot dude who looked like he could wine and dine her then bend her over the arm of the sofa and fuck her good. A twofer. Why not?

Maybe she didn't. Maybe she was in her new place sleeping in her new bed all alone and that's the way she wanted it to be. Without anyone. Without me.

Fine. Fuck it, if that's what she wants. If she wants to be alone – if she wants to be without me – then so be it. I don't need her. I don't need her to smile at me in the morning, make sure we have enough toothpaste, make sure I eat something or at last change my fucking clothes every once in a while. I don't need her to tell me to look for another job since this one sucks, even if it means I have to leave the house because *I should* leave the house because leaving the house and talking to people is a good thing for my soul. I don't need her to tell me she loves me just because, even when I'm not doing anything to make her say that, because I don't need to hear it, to feel it, to be made comfortable in that way. I don't.

I don't.

"Are you seeing that the emails are being quarantined too? I just want to make sure we are in sync before we tell the customer to go to their IT department..."

The voice on the other end of the phone had been speaking for some time, but it had just been background noise until then. I thought I answered this a while ago, before I realized how loud the silence was at o'clock a.m. in my darkened, empty AF house.

"Yeah, that's what I see," I started, spewing out some more bullshit that sounded about right, just enough to satisfy the guy and get him off my back and onto someone else's. I don't need her here to remind me to pay attention to these fucks until I can get the hell out of dodge.

I don't.

ELEVEN

I might need her here to lie to me... to tell me that I'm not losing my mind.

TWELVE

She looked like the slightest movement might make her jump out of her skin.

She was just bringing cookies over, she said. Just wanted to be neighborly, she emphasized by the way she smiled at me from the other side of the open door. But her shifting eyes, peering, squinting, searching the darkness that stood in the corners of my foyer and living room belied a different motive.

The sheriff had come a-callin'.

"I know I should have come again sooner. I guess you were out the first time I stopped by."

I wasn't. I just didn't wanna.

"Good gracious, you've almost been here a year already, haven't you?"

I know she knew exactly how long I've been here. Probably saw me the day we moved in, hefting boxes off the truck, the stress and strain of the process showing in the lines on my face. Probably saw her when she left too – watched her drive off in her car, truck, or whatever she used to haul her stuff away. Bet this biddy could tell me exactly what she was wearing when she came and closed the door on any hope I had of us getting back together.

And no, it hasn't been a fucking year, come on.

"But with all that's been going on, you know, with Pete... oh, it's just so dreadful, isn't it?"

What is?

What??

I still don't know. After all this time, I couldn't figure out how to find out what happened or who was in that body bag after all. I mean, it wasn't like I could just ask someone about it at the next book club meeting or while we mowed our yards. No. Casual banter like that was for people who actually liked other people. Me? Well, there's a reason I mow my lawn when everyone else is eating dinner.

I nodded.

She kept talking.

Of course she did.

"No, couldn't be that long yet," she said, answering her own question, feigning confusion, knowing she could recite the date and time if the right person – or any person – asked her to.

"No, it was still nice out when you and your... well, she isn't here anymore, is she?"

Her voice dipped gravely. I guess she was supposed to sound compassionate but she only ended up sounding conspiratorial.

Silent.

Steady.

Am I smiling?

I hope I am.

I really, really hope I am.

I hope I am giving her my best 'Aw shucks, ma'am, you're right... my girl's been gone for quite some time now' face. The one that mixes chagrin and contrite so well, actors would be envious.

Sniffle.

I sho' do miss her...

The nosy lady peeked around me like I wasn't a real person standing there blocking her view, as if I was just some obstacle, like a vase planted in the middle of a foyer, pretentiously directing foot traffic to orbit around it. I don't know what she was looking for – something she could describe to her friends – probably all street sheriffs like their old buddy here – something that spoke of the miserable life the reclusive neighbor that lived on her street led. She looked but saw nothing because there *was* nothing, nothing at all, nothing, nothing , nothing, and resumed talking again, her smile faltering just the slightest bit.

"Your lady friend," she continued, as if she might be able to make me reply, tell her all the juicy bits she wanted to know. Hesitating, like I really might talk if she just waited me out, she tried again, leading just a little more.

"I don't see her anymore."

I nod.

I grin.

She shifts her weight between her feet.

"Well, anyway, it was nice outside when you moved in. I remember because you were wearing a short-sleeved shirt and I thought, 'what nice arms that young man has'. Yes, it was *warm* out, *really* warm..."

I didn't even hear the rest of what she was saying, not after noticing that strange glint in her eye when she talked about my arms. They may not be much to look at anymore – let yourself go for a while and you lose all those gym muscles fast. But was she, like, *looking* before? Was she looking for someone else, like a niece away at college or a daughter that lived out of state? Or, Christ, was she looking for herself?

Yech!

I could feel my brow furrowing and I tried my best to fix it before she saw. This nice old lady, who probably wasn't as old as I had thought she was at first, was holding out a plate of cookies after all. I don't have to bang her to get them... I just have to play nice.

"I'm sorry, I do go on sometimes," she was saying when I got out of my head and rejoined the conversation. It's what happens when you live alone. You end up talking someone's ear off the moment you get the chance."

She laughed uncomfortably, likely playing the words back in her head and wishing she hadn't uttered them at all.

Silent. Now just to fuck with her.

"Yes, I guess it *has* been a while since you got here, though," she said, determined to right things. "Maybe six months?"

Six months, two weeks, five days, and...

I nod.

She falters.

I let my eyes cascade down to the plate.

Her dog, another little yapper (what's with these people and their affinity for small dogs?) - must have been a Chihuahua or something... little angry mouse - pushed past me and into the shadows of my dining room, taking advantage of her loosening grip on the leash.

"Stu! Stu, come back this instant!"

I turned my head in slow motion watching the leash get swallowed up by the darkness. I could hear the dog panting as he made his way deeper into the house, slowing only to sniff or eye something.

"Stu? Oh, he can be so stubborn sometimes," the woman

said from the door, leaning in to see what was keeping her dog.

I felt the woman move closer to me, but I didn't care about that, not when I could hear the low growls rumbling in the back of the dog's throat, muted but there as they clawed their way to the surface. They almost sounded pained, like something was frightening him, hurting him, doing something to him to elicit the sound.

"Stu?" I said this time, the name as foreign on my lips as my own voice was to my ears after not speaking that much for, well how long was it now, four days? Not since the little girl came to retrieve her frisbee from my lawn and caught me staring out at her from my window. I said hello then but she backed away in fear, the visage of a man dressed in clothes that were entirely too big for his frame waving hi to her from a behind a cloudy window altogether too creepy for her to deal with. It was Friday and it was nice out and I had scared the mess out of a little girl. The rest of work was quiet that day and then there was the weekend and then Monday was quiet too. Sometimes I could go whole days without saying a single word out loud, email and chat working just fine to communicate with work and friends... what little interaction I still had with the people I used to go out for drinks with or watch the occasional game with... which was literally almost nil. If I didn't want to I wouldn't have to utter a sound ever again.

She planted her foot into my foyer, stepping inside gingerly, unsure, hovering in that weird in between that kept her both outside in relative safety and inside in the unknown. She peered around me again, seeing nothing.

"Stu, come on back," I said, calling to the dog again, even as I hear the sounds he's making change - more of a whimper now than a growl.

They sounds were coming from the dining room.

The woman looked at me – I could feel her gaze burning the side of my cheek. She had a look of uneasiness on her face, a little confusion mixed in for good measure. I turned toward her and she didn't expect it, had to stop herself from pulling back. I met her eyes, daring her to ask the questions that were bouncing around in her mind, the ones that wondered why I wanted her dog to get out of my house so much, and why I didn't just walk into the dining room and get him myself.

Because... because...

I looked at her.

She looked at me.

I gave her what I hope was a reassuring smile, but judging from the look on her face, it was not.

"The trash," I started, my voice sounding weak to my own ears, "I missed garbage pick-up this week, so..." I let it dangle. She could infer what she wanted. If more people in this world would just let shit dangle...

"Oh," she said noncommittally. She looked like she didn't believe me, wanted to come inside and discover my stash of what, exactly? What did she think I was hiding in there... drugs? Sex toys? Whatever. If she called bullshit, would I take her in there, let her see...?

The dog whimpered loudly this time, a sharp, biting thing that sounded like a fear response more than anything else. Like his back was against the wall.

She lurched all the way into the house calling Stu's name as she made her way inside, the cookie plate falling from her hands to clatter against the floor, splintering, fracturing against the hardwood, little pieces of porcelain embedding themselves in the chocolate chips. I grabbed her arm and yanked her back, pulling, damn near throwing her until she was several paces behind me because... because there was something she shouldn't... something *no* one should...

"I got it," I said firmly, my tone maybe a little too hostile for the situation. The lady was only concerned about her dog, after all. But still, this is my house and I don't need anybody poking around in it...

"But...?" she said, her eyes pleading, but I shut that shit down. People always said I have a killer glare and with the look I cut her, I guess I do.

"Stu?" she resorted to, calling for the dog again once it was clear she wasn't getting any further.

It only took a couple of seconds – five at the most – for my world to be turned upside down.

One Mississippi...

Stu barked futilely, sounding like his end was drawing near, like he was begging for mercy.

Two Mississippi...

I turned back to the dining room and called the dog's name in chorus with the old biddy, taking a wide step toward the room's entryway.

Three Mississippi...

Stu found his balls and started growling , his deep utterings reverberating off the walls.

Four Mississippi...

The biddy exclaimed in a mix of surprise, happiness, and fear at the same moment that I furrowed my brows in worry.

Five Mississippi...

Stu backed out of the dining room like a shot, tugging something along with him... something big and discolored, something dirty and wet...

"Stu!"

The biddy moved then, arms outstretched and wanting at seeing her dog emerge from the shadows, his appearance somehow ungluing her from the spot in the foyer. I moved too, fast as lightening, faster than I have moved in months, and made it to the dog first. I looked at what he was tugging out of the darkness. My subconscious connected the dots before my conscious could, saw the gray, waxen, log-like, gnawed thing before it even registered as real to my senses and promptly sent the signal to kick the thing away before scooping the dog up.

Stu yelped.

Stu snapped at me.

It took everything I had not to break Stu's little neck.

The biddy was on me.

"Oh! Oh, Stu!" she exclaimed, snatching her dog out of my arms and looking at him closely. I wonder what it had looked like from where she was standing. Did she think I had kicked her dog? Did she see the thing I dislodged from its greedy little mouth?

"Oh, baby, you gave me a fright!"

Hmmm. A fright. Maybe she *was* old.

"You can't just run off like that!" she continued, cooing to the dog like it could understand her. To me she said, "I'm so sorry. Stu never acts like that. He- he's never bitten anyone in his whole life."

"And he still hasn't," I assured her, as I made my way to where she stood and rested a hand on her shoulder, preparing to usher her out. This earned me a pretty impressive snarl from Stu.

"Bad boy!" she admonished but Stu was undeterred. His eyes darted between me and the darkened hallway where the thing he was dragging out, the thing that suddenly I could smell and it was dank and metallic and curiously woodsy like rotted leaves, sat waiting in the darkness.

Me.

The thing.

The thing?

The *arm...*?

"Oh dear, I've made a terrible mess," she said as she looked at the broken plate and the ruined cookies. I wanted to say, 'Hell yeah, you made a mess! The broom is in the closet,' but now was not the time. I needed them out. O-U-T... OUT, and right now. I needed to see what the hell Stu had gotten into in the corner of my dining room, where there were always shadows.

I needed to see what he had dragged back with him.

"It's fine," I purred, placating her the way I did my customers when they called me before dawn. "I'm only sorry I won't get to taste your cookies now."

"Oh, I'll bring more by another day," she said as she stepped over the threshold, her face registering relief as soon as she was safely outside. She said she would, but she really didn't want to – the apprehension that shone in her eyes was proof of that. It was just the expected response and I have to give it to her; it was pretty ballsy to stick to protocol after being scared shitless.

She was still clutching Stu.

Stu didn't seem to have a problem with that.

"If you don't mind...?" Laying on the charm before I slam the door in her nosy face.

"No, no, it's no bother," she said, her voice trailing off as she peered around me almost involuntarily.

Could she see it?

I had the fight the urge to turn around and have a look myself.

"Thank you," I said, my tone decidedly dismissive. "Well, I need to get back. I've got a call this afternoon that I need to prepare for."

Lies, all lies.

"Oh yes, that's right. You work from home."

"Mhmm."

"What is it you do, again? Customer service, or-"

"Project management," I corrected, even though I knew it might start another conversation.

"Right, yes. For what company, again? I seem to recall hearing something about-"

"Technology," I said, cutting her off. The hell if I was telling her who I worked for. Why would she need to know that? Did she want to look the company up, maybe figure out how much I make? Next we'd be painting our nails together and talking about our first times.

Fuck no.

The stench in the house was unbearable now. I was sure she could smell it even with the scent of my neighbor Bob's freshly cut grass in the air.

"I'm sorry, I really do have to go," I said, closing the door slowly, hoping she would get the hint before I slammed it shut in her face.

"Ok then. I-I'll bring the cookies by another time. I promise I'll keep both hands on the plate this time and leave Stu at home."

She laughed self-deprecatingly.

I laughed along with her... it's the only thing I *could* do.

She smiled.

So did I.

The sound of the door closing was the biggest relief of my life.

I turn back to the dining room, fear pushing through my veins, threatening to freeze me in place like the biddy had been moments before. I took a step, porcelain crunching underfoot as I moved toward the darkness.

The room is still so dark, inky almost... I guess I never got around to doing much with the blinds in the house Still, it shouldn't be so dark back there in the middle of the day.

There's something on the floor.

Sure there is, my subconscious tried. *There has to be, unless you* are *some kind of sadistic fuck who kicks at little dogs for fun.*

Sometimes that voice in my head worked, knocked me out of whatever sour mood I was settling into, but not this time. This time the levity it so often offered up, dripping with sarcasm just the way I liked it, didn't even make me crack a smile.

I crept toward the thing on the floor, cocked my head to the side to peek at it, squinted my eyes to distinguish it from the blackness I was engulfed by, all the while not wanting to look at it head on. I was afraid I would see it, truly see it, and it wouldn't be hard to figure out what it was at all, not hard to see the shape of a forearm, the shadow of delicate fingers.

Her fingers.

My heart seized in my chest and I stopped dead in my tracks, my dingy robe billowing around my ankles. Could that really be what was in there? Her...?

I was so angry... so fucking angry that she walked out and left me the way she did. She didn't even have the decency to have a proper fight about it. She just... left. Why was it so easy to leave me standing there holding the bag, to walk away from everything we had built, everything we had planned?

I had been angry, yes, but had I been angry enough to... to...

There was something there, on the floor, light against the dark, muted... gray. Highlighted against the darkness, standing out, *sticking* out...

Pulsating.

Writhing, distorting, undulating... moving.

It was moving.

I didn't recognize the gasp, audible in its raspiness but muted, formless, subsumed by the heavy air around me, but it was mine, that much I knew. It came from me, was made by me in a last effort to shock myself into motion. And it worked. I unstuck myself like a statue finding that its legs actually worked and lunged for the light switch on the wall behind me, barely touching it with my outstretched fingers as I fell to the floor in an uncoordinated heap, but purchase was purchase.

The light came on to reveal an empty dining room. Nothing on the floor, on the walls, or anywhere.

My fingers hurt; one of them had bent backwards on the switch.

So did the knee that I had fallen squarely on like a sack of potatoes as I flailed.

My mind still wanted to retreat, to back away from the room that I had fallen at the mouth of, just barely on the safe side of the pillars that separated the dining room and living room. But there was no need to run, nothing to be afraid of at all, right? Because there was nothing there.

Nothing at all.

And then it *was* there on the floor beneath the windowsill.

No, it was there in the spot where the curio was supposed to go.

No, that's not right because there it was in the middle of the room, gray fingers with blackened fingertips scratching at the carpet, push pull, push pull, crawling toward me...

I blinked.

It was gone.

What the hell is happening to me?

My heart rate is slowing but my mind picked up the baton and started sprinting to the finish. Why am I seeing these things? Why now?

Nothing there, nothing there.

If there was nothing there, what did that dog have in his mouth?

What was that putrid smell that hung in the air, cloying even now, making my throat close?

What have I done to –

The cellphone rang, insistent, obnoxious thing that it is and for once, I was happy it did.

THIRTEEN

A Chinese guy and Indian guy go into a bar...
It started innocently enough - just your usual conference call with Dev and Ops duking it out over a hotfix and the timing of the application of said hotfix and the backout plan should said hotfix not work. But, of course, that would never happen, said Dev, because after all, they created the foolproof hotfix. Garden variety topic in the IT world, one that any project manager worth their salt knows they can zone out of for at least the first 20 minutes if they wanted to. And that's what I intended to do: zone out. Read an article online, maybe try to figure out what color #thedress really was – anything to kill time. But then, as my grandfather would have said, 'Up jump the devil!', an argument worthy of a laugh track started. That I struggled to understand most of it made it even better.

The developer was Chinese and he started off politely, talking about the hotfix and why it needed to be done right away. The operations guy was Indian and was not happy about the timing- not happy at all. I wasn't happy either, but not for the same reasons. They were both in the middle of their workday, seeing the sun shine from their window, tossing a Nerf ball at a makeshift basketball hoop, but it was the middle of the night for me. I was none too pleased at the prospect of having to sit up for hours waiting for the damned thing to burn in, but I said nothing – I never got a chance to.

Indian guy said no.

Chinese guy said yes.

It went back and forth like this for a while – common fare so far.

But then the Chinese guy got angry and started swearing in his language. At least I think he was swearing – he said whatever he said emphatically, hotly, like the words stung his lips on their way out. The Indian guy heard the tone and asked what he said. Told him to say it again, but this time in English. The Chinese guy went silent. And then the Indian guy made the sound, that not so subtle expelling of breath, that *hmph* that universally means, 'yeah, I didn't think so' just loud enough so we could all hear it.

Challenged, the Chinese guy lost his shit and went off on a diatribe that was CNN and Fox News-worthy, but he did it in his language. The Indian guy responded in kind, at least I think he did because it was in *his* language. Hindi versus Mandarin or was it Bengali versus Cantonese – whichever it was - English, the lingua franca, be damned. They spoke at the same time, loudly, sometimes pausing for effect, sometimes sounding like they were issuing threats. I almost spit the sip of my fourth cup of coffee, the one that was piping hot and that I had just slurped unceremoniously into my mouth, out - nearly sprayed it like you see on sitcoms when they started banging on their desks to emphasize their words...

words that no one on the call understood... not even their intended targets. It wasn't just because it was happening at some ungodly hour of night – the shit was funny. I would have contributed to a pot to continue this thing in a ring in some neural territory if someone had suggested it: it was that good. Imagine it: *all the way from Mumbai, in the red corner is* – cue Michael Buffer's voice – *Maaaaaanojjjjj!. And in the blue corner, all the way from Hong Kong, Llllllleeeeeeeeee! Let's get ready to rumble!* And the crowd goes wild!

I was so busy laughing to myself about the prospect of a head-to-head match, so busy listening to them fight and then hearing the NOC guy try to interject to get things back on track – it would be awesome if he was wearing a blue button-up shirt with black pants and a bowtie, just like they do on televised boxing matches...– that I didn't see her coming.

And she was coming. She was coming fast.

Pale, everything pale. Bluish gray. Translucent.

Dead.

She was dead and she was coming, coming towards me with a speed she had never possessed in life. She was coming and I had nowhere to run, nowhere to hide sitting at my desk the way I am. My back is to the wall and my huge wooden monstrosity of a workspace is facing the door. There is only a small space on one side to get out – the other side is too close to the wall. I had been careless when I set the room up, sliding the desk into place just eager to call it done, really. I'd been meaning to correct that, to make the space on the sides of the desk a little more even, but, you know, with my busy schedule and all... Leaving it lopsided meant I only had one way to escape her – the massive desk, which had been her idea, interestingly enough, effectively pinned me in.

She came fast and low, army crawling toward me, her

black eyes trained on mine. Her hair was stringy and limp, pasted to her face in places, as though she was wet. Her face was featureless, the pallor of death taking away any distinguishing marks, laugh lines, signs of animation. Her mouth was emotionless and I was thankful for that, because her eyes did enough damage. They were all black.

Empty.

Bottomless pits.

The cornea and sclera were gone to waste leaving a cavernous nothingness that still seemed to stare at me, to suck me in.

She was naked. Her body stuck to the floor in places as her arms and legs propelled her forward, ripping off skin and muscle along the way, but I had no time to the consider the carnage in her wake because... because...

"But I didn't hurt you... I didn't... I wouldn't have done anyth-..."

Her stopping her charge was almost worse than her covering ground toward me at such a rapid pace. At least when she was coming toward me I didn't have time to think, time to feel anything other than terror. But now that she had stopped, now that she had pulled herself up to stand, her face breaking into the emotion it had been devoid of before, there was *too much* time to see, to feel... to ache.

Her brow furrowed as she heard my babbled words, head turned to the side, lips downturned in sadness. I wanted to touch her cheek, to reassure her that whatever had befallen her hadn't been at my hands, but I thought if I felt the coldness of her skin beneath my fingers I might go crazy. She looked away from me, into the dining room, then back at me imploringly.

"What happened, baby?" I heard myself say, my own

head tilting as I looked at her, my sweetheart, dead dead dead in the doorway of my office.

She looked like she was about to cry, her face contorting into the telltale posture of squinting eyes and pouty lips until she opened her mouth wider than was humanly possible and screamed.

FOURTEEN

I sleep at my desk too much.

There's something about the light coming off computer monitors that isn't right and it's fucking with me. That's all it is, pure and simple. It's confusing me. Bewildering me. I don't know what to call it, but something is definitely happening and it has got to stop. Maybe I'm not getting enough REM sleep or deep sleep or whatever kind of sleep is the one you're supposed to get the most of. Whatever it is, it is screwing with my head.

When I woke up at my desk that next morning and several mornings since, I checked the dining room. Not right away, of course, and not without feeling like I might shit my pants before getting there, but I made myself do it and there's nothing there. No dismembered arm lying haphazardly on the cream carpet. No body sitting in a plastic bag propped up against the wall, its eyes looking at me from some special place in Hell. No stain the color of brackish water waiting for me, smelling of sulfur and rot, indelible in the carpet fiber, the paint on the walls.

There was nothing at all.

I don't know why that dog sniffing around – like dogs do...? – made me think that my ex-fiancée, my *dead* ex-fiancée was around the corner waiting to reach out and touch me. All I know is that people sleep prone in actual beds for a reason, not bent in half, ass in a chair, arms and head on a table.

So today, after I picked my head up off my desk, the line of spit that connected my cheek to it snapping in mid-air, I decided that things were going to change around here.

I had never actually set the bed up.

We had a mattress when we moved in and that was on the floor stripped of matching sheets and a proper comforter because she had taken every damned thing when she snuck in that day. We had been waiting for the new bedframe and headboard to deliver when we called it quits. If she had just told me she wanted out a few weeks earlier, I could have saved a pretty penny on all the extra shit I bought for our new life, the bed – the whole damned house – included.

The bed frame was in the corner separated into a few sealed boxes... still. The mattress had a wayward top sheet on it in a tangle, like I had fought to get out one morning as it desperately tried to trip me up and keep me in. There was no fitted sheet – I don't even know if I have one anymore. The pillow had no pillowcase. The blanket was balled up at one end – hardly on the bed at all. Empty chip bags and plastic shopping bags were strewn all over the place. I don't even think I was this disjointed – this sloppy – in college. It was like a crackhouse in there.

I couldn't help thinking about what my mom would say if she saw the pigsty that was my life. Only she wouldn't see it. She lived too far away to pop in for a visit. Even when she had been a snowbird, fleeing the North for the smothering warmth of Florida as soon as the air caught the slightest of chills, she wouldn't have just driven by unannounced. I have always been thankful for that. One overheard moan was, apparently, enough for the both of us. And now she had made Florida, the sauna that it is, her permanent residence, so no, she wouldn't be able to just pop over and see the squalor I'm living in. Squalor of my own doing. Neither would my friends. Wives, girlfriends, kids, work – all that shit took precedence now, whether we liked it or not. We weren't in college anymore; we couldn't fuck around all day watching football and drinking beer. Now we have errands to run on our days off, shit to fix or buy, babies to play with... at least they do.

I wish it hadn't but my mind went back to the shitstorm that was my life now. *I* was supposed to have all of that now, was supposed to have turned the page and started a new chapter, one where wedding bells would sound and babies would giggle. I had always assumed I would have those things eventually, always figured I'd be just like everybody else. But life moved on without me... left me standing in the middle of the rubbish it left behind.

And now I'm waxing philosophical.

I really need to get my shit together.

I looked at the bed and all the garbage on top of and around it but had a new focus now. Something crunched when I pushed a ball of socks that looked suspiciously like a rat king to the side, clearing a space to lay down. I needed room for what had to be done now, and I didn't want any left-over Doritos crumbles on my ass when all was said and done.

Sigh. It's been entirely too long since I've done this.

My dick and I used to have an agreement. We would see each other every few days if there hadn't been any other action – three days tops, but that was really pushing it. But now, since she left, since the 3 am conference calls started, since every time I get in the shower, go to cook something, take a piss, the fucking phone starts blaring, well, it's been a while. Two weeks? A month? Longer? Shit, I really don't know.

What I do know is that my hand feels good as shit right now.

Warm.

Sure.

Capable.

Fuck, I better slow down.

The orgasm will come – it always does. I know how to do me best... and right now, it wouldn't take much. But I didn't just want to beat one off real fast. I wanted to feel it, tease myself, wake my body up. Maybe after this I'll go out and take that damned walk I've been thinking about taking. Wash this shitty robe or better yet, throw this bitch out and get a new one. Open the goddamned blinds so the shadows aren't so heavy in the house... in the dining room...

My hand ran up the length of my shaft, encircled the head and gave a little squeeze, reminded me what was important here.

My eyes fluttered shut as I found my rhythm. I had to fight to keep my hips from bucking because they wanted to – I wanted them to – but I needed to slow it down, stretch it out.

Breathe.

Fucking breathe.

On the beach, the sun kissing random girl's copper skin. Latina? Middle Eastern? Caribbean? She looks a little like Rihanna...? Wherever the fuck she's from... pretty eyes, full lips. She blows a kiss, no... she kisses at me... licks her lips...

I bite my own bottom lip.

She's laying down, legs open...

show me...pretty...

My hips buck, unrestrained now, chasing my hand, chasing my high.

She moans.

I fucking grunt, it feels so good.

Tight in my stomach. My toes curl as my legs go stiff...

Cold.

On my hand.

On my dick.

Cold.

So cold it almost burns.

My eyes fly open to see and I wish they hadn't... I wish I hadn't...

Stroking me to the head, twisting her wrist like I like, dead, dead, make me come...

I screamed. Even as the coil in my stomach gave way and I came all over the dirty moth-bitten undershirt that I forgot to move out of the way, I screamed. She had me... she had me... and she wouldn't let go.

Cum on her dead fingers. Her black tongue darted out of her mouth to lick it up.

FIFTEEN

I didn't kill her.

I didn't fucking kill her.

I don't know how long I've been in my office telling myself this, but it's true. It has to be. She walked out of here on her own two feet, railing against me about every little thing I had ever done to her or *not* done, which was, apparently, more of the problem. Cursing, screaming, stomping, but of her own volition. I remember it like it was yesterday even though I keep trying like hell to forget it. So why do I keep seeing her here, hiding in the shadows, her skin grayish blue with wet hair sticking to her forehead and cheeks? Why does she stare back at me with eyes like black holes, peering at me like I'm some alien life form that she has never seen before? Why the hell does she keep looking into my soul with the deadest eyes, more devoid of life than any living being's could possibly be?

I don't think I can stand another night of being afraid of the darkness or what's crawling toward me from the dining room.

I look at my cell, cue up her number from my contact list, and get ready to call. All that stands between me and her right now is that little green phone icon, but my thumb just won't push it, won't press down. It's not like she can break my heart again - it hasn't reconstituted itself from the first time. It's not like she can tell me how much of an awful person I am and have it mean anything anymore – she already told me what she thinks of me and that's fine. It's just... what if she sounds happy? What if she sounds like she's answering the phone from the shore of a beach where she's having a picnic with her new boyfriend? What if she sounds like she was in the middle of laughing at the best joke she had ever heard, one that might even be at my expense. *'Oh, there's your loser ex on the phone, probably gonna beg for you to come back, wah wah wah...'*

I don't even know if a new boyfriend exists yet and I'm ready to wipe that self-righteous smirk off of dude's face already.

So, call. Hear her voice. All she has to do is say hello and you can hang up. It's not like you need to have a conversation with her, find out how she's doing where she is right now and with who. All you need to do is hear her voice and put this horror show to bed.

Right.

My thumb is shaking. It is hovering over the green phone icon and its shaking.

There's a wet sounding *schthwack* in the back of my mind... muted, like a memory.

I smash the call button, fear more than determination propelling me forward.

I want to check the dining room real quick, but I'm afraid to.

Ring.

Ring.

Ring.

Schthwack

Ring.

Ring.

Sch-

Hi, it's me and I'm out doing something. Leave a message and I'll call back.

I waited for the rest of the *schthwack* to come, waited for the arm to slap down on the floor again, its gelatinous membrane sticking to the fibers, very much like glaze on a donut.

I waited for it to happen, for it to make that sound, to send the scent of death, that mix of earthen rot and sweetness that is so pungent it can permeate your dreams. I waited, glued in place as the thing in the dining room, came closer, closer, ever closer...

But it didn't.

Nothing happened.

The voicemail message ended and the tone beeped. I left one of those annoying messages that are mostly silent but you can hear something in the background – maybe breathing, maybe change rustling... *something* – but, infuriatingly, no one speaks. And then I hung up.

No closure.

No.

Closure.

I could almost imagine a raspy laugh issuing from her ruined throat.

"They wouldn't leave her voicemail on if she was dead," I reasoned aloud to the empty room, my voice embarrassingly tinny. But wouldn't they? What if she had just died... no one is thinking about cancelling bills right after someone dies, are they? And didn't you hear stories about people calling their loved ones' voicemails just to hear their voice for years to come? I saw my grandmother call her friend's phone number for months after she died, just letting the phone ring until the voicemail engaged. It scared the hell out of her when someone picked up the other end of the line one day, considering her friend had lived alone for 15 years. Her son had finally gotten around to turning off the lights and the phone and giving up the apartment, so someone else was the owner of that phone number now, Mrs. Claudette's voice forever gone. But that was months after her death, after the son had healed enough to handle the business of closing out her affairs. So yeah, if she had just died it was possible that her phone still worked and her voicemail was attached. Even if I killed her before she could walk out the door, it might not be out of the realm of possibility that –

What?

No!

I *didn't* kill her!

Maybe someone else did, but I didn't.

Wait, did someone kill her?

Is she... is the woman I had planned to spend the rest of my life with dead?

Why did I think that?

Why had I just assumed she was dead, just let that become the truth in my mind?

Maybe she's not even dead.

She is *not* dead.

If she's not dead, what was goin-...?

Why wouldn't she answer? Maybe because she was out fucking some guy? Mr. Perfect who is on track to being partner at the law firm he works at, builds houses with

Habitat for Humanity in his spare time, and rescues puppies. Sure, why not?

But no, that wasn't true was it... because she's dead, isn't she?

I couldn't stop my mind from bouncing around, landing on one scenario only to give up and perch on the next as though trying it on for size. My thumb hovered over the green phone icon again, waiting for my command.

The phone was heavy in my hand.

She is **not** dead...

... right?

I clicked the three little dots on the side of the screen and selected Delete.

I shouldn't even have her phone number taking up space in my contacts anymore.

SIXTEEN

The sun is incredibly bright today. Inordinately so, almost like it's a fireball hanging in the sky right over my house.

How long has it been since I've looked outside?

The flowers are in bloom – I can smell the lavender in the garden next door. Spring is here, hooray and all that jazz.

The sun is hella bright and hot as hell.

I feel it burning my skin through my tattered robe as I scamper out to pick up my groceries. The heat was uncomfortable, yet it gave me pause. I took stock of myself in that moment, my disheveled appearance, my overgrown nails and smelly pajama bottoms. The scurrying around, determined to spend as little time in the world as possible. The jitteriness. The solitude. When had I started living on the periphery like this, using the shadows as cover as I darted in and out of the sun like it might burn me? Was it when I said, 'fuck the supermarket' and started ordering my groceries online because who the hell needed another encounter with the cheese lady? Was it when I said, 'fuck shopping for clothes –

Amazon has everything I need'? Was it when I started streaming all my movies and reading Twitter for my news?

Maybe.

Possibly.

Probably.

This can't be healthy.

I dropped the groceries off in the kitchen – never did get a dog, so no table-surfing nose would snot all over the food – and went right upstairs, did not pass go or collect $200, and made a beeline for my closet. I didn't allow myself to stand there forever, staring at the clothes with glazed-over eyes – think long, think wrong, right? I just picked out a t-shirt and jeans that used to fit well but were decidedly snug now, and got out of the house, smoothing the wayward strands of my hair down as I went.

Warm.

The air felt warm on my face, my bare arms. I wore a t-shirt out today, not because I wanted to show of my pale arms or atrophied muscles, not even because I wanted to feel the warmth on said neglected limbs, but because everyone else would be wearing short-sleeved shirts and the last thing I want to do was stick out like a sore thumb. It had been so long since I'd been outside that people were already going to either wonder who the hell the new guy was or why the hermit from down the street had ventured out of his house today of all days.

I shut the door, made it out onto my steps, then onto my walkway.

And froze.

What the hell?

I tried to tell myself to move, to get going, to stop standing there, eyes wide like a deer in the headlights, but I just couldn't move.

What was going on?

It wasn't like I was agoraphobic... it had just been a while.

So, why couldn't I move? Why did it feel like people were staring at me, watching me stand there looking like a fish out of water, from their windows? Why did it seem like the trees, the houses, the very air was closing in on me, suffocating me, trying to make me...

... what? Frightened?

Nervous?

Pay?

The mere thought of that last word and what it could mean dislodged the clog that seemed to have been down my throat, blocking my airway, trying to make me gag. It was almost like the realization of what was gone – the base understanding of the truth – was enough to set me back in motion, to make me move ahead and walk, maybe even right down to the police station to turn myself in.

What?

I turned back to the house, sure I heard something there... the end of a chuckle dying in the wind... a clicking in the back of the throat...

I stumbled backwards then turned toward the street and had to resist the urge to run. Steeling myself, I reached the end of my walkway keeping to a casual pace that nearly drove me mad and turned right, toward the park, never looking back for fear that I might see her waiting for me in the doorway.

I tried to clear my mind with every step - right, then left... right, then left - until it actually worked and I was walking, I was enjoying the day just like everyone else. And it was good. The fresh air felt good, *smelled* good. The flowers looked pretty – red and yellow and purple tulips lining the entrance to the community park against a backdrop of evergreen hedges that were taller than I am. But it wasn't just that. It was the whole idea of being outside that was good. The nature – fucking birds chirping overhead! – the gurgling of the water fountain somewhere inside the park, the laughter of children and they ran around in circles, the easy banter of the people strolling by. Life – it was good and I was happy to be out there living it. Happy to see other people and smile at them and maybe say hello. Happy to be out there instead of inside in the dark, always so damned dark in there, even on a day like this. Happy to just be.

Yeah, I've been inside too long.

I mean, it's easy to do – the way things are these days, you don't have to go outside for anything at all if you don't want to. And I haven't wanted to, not for a long time. I got my groceries online, my music online, my porn online. I watched movies, television, read the news, bought boxers, even gambled online when I wanted to. I work online – I am convinced now that working from home is nothing more than a big conference bridge that you jump on and off of as needed – talk to people online courtesy of Skype. There hadn't been a reason to go outside... except that my skin had taken on an unnatural pallor and my eyes were still trying to adjust to the daylight as if they had never encountered it before.

It was time.

The park was full. People playing touch football; people flying kites; moms pushing strollers; kids on the monkey bars. There was a group of people lined up behind easels staring at a tree, their paint party going "on location" instead of staying cooped up in some bar smelling of old beer. There were kids playing soccer, boys mostly, except for the goalie who, since I had been walking around the shrub-lined walkway near them, hadn't allowed the other team to score yet.

I took a deep breath and was surprised to enjoy the way it coursed through my body, clean and light and so very different from the heavy dust-filled muck I sucked in from my desk every day.

Life was happening here. Thanks for the invitation to the party...

... because Cindy... she wouldn't be able to enjoy something as simple as a breath of fresh air anymore, would she? She was dead and almost in the ground.

... and Tyler probably loved this warm weather because it gave him an excuse that his wife would believe when he wants to go out with the girl he met at the gas station.

Hmm.

With a tilt of the head, I sat down on the bench, wondering what all that was about. I watched people go by and felt my mind toiling away, crafting backstories for them. Horrible, depraved narratives, the kind of lives you wouldn't wish on your enemies. I chastised myself, told myself not to engage in the new pastime my mind seemed to take up every time I tried to go out and be a part of the world, to exist in the land of the living... every time I tried to be normal. I told myself no... not this time.

Dogs on leashes pulling their owners because a butterfly crossed their path and they wanted to investigate.

Girls skipping rope along the path even as their mothers told them to let the people walking along the path by.

A man sitting on a bench across from him with a newspaper in his lap.

An old woman knitting a blanket, the needles too big in her hands, her tears blood red on her cheeks.

I gasped.

The little boy chasing pigeons in front of my bench looked at me out of the corner of his eye, but then went back to the business of clearing the path of any and all of the filthy birds, his lips twisted into a snarl.

My heart thumped in my chest, felt like it was trying to break through my skin to escape. I hadn't realized that I had looked away from the boy, forced my eyes to take in something else, until I saw the man shake the creases out of his newspaper, that obnoxious habit that readers of that archaic medium insisted upon nurturing. They're all, 'Look at me! Look at me! I'm reading an actual newspaper and have the dirty fingertips to prove it, unlike you uncultured trolls who get your news online!'. But that gentle shuffle of papers sobered me up enough to come back to the moment, feel the wind on my face and the bench under my ass. I took a deep breath and let it out slow, then did it all over again. And then I found my balls and looked at the old lady again. She was still there, wasn't some apparition haunting me in the broad daylight – because every self-respecting ghost knows that they own the night and should leave the daytime to lesser creatures like witches and, I don't know... maybe dragons – but she didn't have knitting needles the size of marine bolts in her hands this time and she wasn't crying blood. But her over-stuffed yarn bag, the one that sat innocently on the bench next to her, most definitely contained a human head.

The teenager riding the scooter along the path? His lips were stained red from the blood he'd consumed at his mother's neck.

The rocking chairs in the cozy corner of the park, the ones nestled among the trees enjoying the best shade the park had to offer? Two of them swayed as if moved by a couple enjoying the sun on a beautiful spring day, while the other two were still. The chairs were empty. There was no breeze to speak of.

The kids, covered head to toe in sand and cat feces deposited by the local feral population overnight, were busy little archaeologists, dusting of debris to uncover the bone and beak of a cassowary.

What the fuck? What the actual fuck??

I stood up nervously, my legs moving of their own volition, getting me walking, moving, escaping the madness. The woman with the knitting needles looked up, her watery blue eyes smiling behind thick-framed glasses to match the bright, dentured one on her mouth as a child ran toward her giggling with an Icee in hand.

Double Dutch. A girl leading in and jumping in rhythm. Fire. One rope is on fire. The other is made of snakes.

A wet slurping behind me as I turned and ran for the exit, nevermind the old men playing dominoes, one obviously dead and the other very much alive and outfitted with a party hat and silly glasses – the kind with lenses that were white and black swirls designed to hypnotize you if you looked too close. Nevermind the cow grazing in the patch of grass near the entrance to the park, a horn sticking out of its forehead like a rhinoceros.

I ran, turning up blocks that weren't familiar, seeing cars that would put Cuba's classics to shame, hoping to God that I would find my way back home, back inside, where no one could hurt me. Except maybe...

The sun is warm and the air smells oh so sweet.

Note to self: Fuck going outside.

SEVENTEEN

"We will have to reconvene at 1:00 a.m. EST to execute the emergency change," I heard through my laptop's speakers, the lilt in the woman's voice pleasant even though the words she spoke I could have done without. "We will set up individual customer bridges to brief them as we go along."

We.

It always strikes me as funny when they say 'we', like it was a group effort. Like they were going to help in the process of both doing the fix and talking with the customers, who would be royally pissed the whole way through the call, even if the change actually alleviates the pain they were feeling. Why? Because they had to do it in the first place. Because the product they bought wasn't working and they had to run reports and have meetings and watch shit trickle down onto them from the executive levels before they could pass said shit on to the vendor, people like me. An application like this should just work without having to be played with as much as we do, compliance checks and updates aside. *That's* why they would be mad. Because by the time we get this emergency change in place, they would have endured days of failed patches, failed workarounds, and bullshit excuses. And the bad thing is, they know we'll be back in the same boat in about a week when something else goes to shit.

"Ok, then, get some rest and we'll get back on at 1:00 o'clock."

There were a bunch of 'oks' and 'thank yous' before people hung up. I even heard myself saying one of those as I signed off the call and tried to prepare myself for what was to come. 1 a.m.. It was only 4:00 p.m. I still have an hour to work (well, an hour that I am *supposed* to work, but let's be real for a moment, shall we? There will be some call to attend, some issue to resolve, some document to finish that will keep me sitting here for likely another three hours.), so getting some rest is out of the question, isn't it? And then there's dinner to make and eat. By the time I start feeling tired enough to actually get some sleep, it'll be about an hour or so before the bridge started up again. Naps are not beneficial when real sleep is what your body actually wants. Waking up right after your body settles into sleep is akin to torture.

I wonder if there is a form of torture being used by some military faction somewhere that is based solely on sleep deprivation like that, the kind where they let you think you'll be allowed to sleep, only to wake you up with a loud, blaring noise.

But I digress.

I do that sometimes, just let my mind wander off, because it is easier to do that than to face what is really going on.

Because it is still going on, no matter how much I would like to think it is over – to think that it was all a figment of my imagination and that she really is still alive and well somewhere on the other side of town, in another state, on the other side of the world. I don't know if that is true anymore. I don't know how it can be.

I went onto her Facebook and she has unfriended me... of course she did... but she did that before walking out the door. Made a big stink about it when she did it, clicking the button in some grand, over-exaggerated gesture, like that was supposed to hurt me. I didn't give a shit – she's the one who lives and breathes social media. I prefer things old school, you know - going out for drinks and NOT taking a picture of it or taking a selfie in front of it or tagging my location. When you see those posts with a caption that says, 'Hey, come join me!'... I mean, do *you* ever go? Do you ever drop what you're doing to meet the person out and enjoy the evening? Never! You probably look at those posts and smile and it's a heinous little smile too, isn't it? One that is full of disdain and judgement and outright meanness. *Needy*, your mind likely quips. *Desperate for company, huh? Well, not me. I am just fine sitting here in my pjs looking at your pictures from the comfort of my own home.* I liked to live life instead of watching everyone else do it, that is, until life started to turn on me, seeing something in my face and hating it, biting me in the ass every chance it got.

She hadn't posted in months... but that's just what us uninitiated folks who were not on her Friends list could see.

And anyway, what did that mean? I hadn't posted in even longer.

I don't have Instagram or Snapchat accounts for her to unfollow and only look at Twitter for the news; two social media outlets to keep up with were more than enough for me. I can't remember what her username was on either of those to try to find her, got mentally tired even trying to think of what silly thing she might call herself, so I stopped. Which means I still don't really know anything.

Shrill ringing filled the air, echoing off the walls that I still haven't put anything on yet.

"Please get on the conference bridge I just sent you credentials for." – no 'hello', no 'sorry to disturb you'... no pretense at all from the frazzled voice on the other end of the line.

What email?

Ding.

Ah, yes, that email, the one that just came in... after the phone call asking me to hurry up and get on.

Told you... it didn't even take a full 10 minutes.

Twenty of us this time, different people from before, but the same underlying problem. Hard at work right away talking about what the customer experience is and what steps we can take to mitigate the current problem before actually trying to figure out why it happened again. I should write down my script and recycle it for every one of these conversations. Maybe I should record myself and just play it when these calls come up. I wonder if anyone would even notice.

Wouldn't she have a memorialized Facebook page if she was dead?

How do you get one of those? Would someone have to contact Facebook and pay for one or does your page turn into one automatically? It can't be automatic – This isn't *The Hunger Games*... a chime doesn't go off after you die, alerting anyone bothering to watch the broadcast that you have turned in your timecard. But then how would they find out you were dead? I bit my lip as I answered my own question.

A loved one might would have to tell them. Maybe a significant other.

I went back to Facebook, back to her page and it looked normal. It didn't have that melancholy funeral home verbiage on it; there was no talk of lost ones and whatnot – it didn't say 'Remembering' next to her name. So, maybe...

But did that mean...

I don't know whether to be happy about this development or not. No memorial page could mean she was alive and well. But it could also mean that she didn't have a significant other to create one. If the job had been left to her mother, the people in Hell asking for ice water would have a better chance of getting satisfaction than that page ever had of seeing the light of day. Or maybe her significant other was like him and just didn't give a shit about Facebook...

People have "types" they are attracted too, right?

"The process continues to fail after a certain number of attempts..."

Cue the recording, "Can we set the threshold to clear attempts before failure occurs?" I think I have asked this question four times in the past few days. So much so, that I can recite what their answer will be. Maybe they have written their scripts down already.

Dead or alive?

Dead or alive?

I just wish there was some way I could figure it out that didn't involve any potential interaction with her 'loved ones'. You know, like her mother or, God forbid, the significant other...

When the wet slapping on the hardwood floor made its way to my ears I couldn't help thinking, *Ask and you will receive.*

Close.

So very close.

Over the carpet in the dining room and through the living room, to slap against the wood floor in the foyer.

Pretty much right outside the door to my office.

EIGHTEEN

Nine years.

Nine years of studying for certification tests, getting bitched out by customers who wanted updates on the hour, no, on the *half* hour, carpal tunnel, and countless interrupted dates.

Nine years of emergency meetings, PowerPoint slides, and lack of sleep.

Nine years of building a career, proving my worth, 'maintaining customer relationships' - isn't that the new term for kissing the ass of the people who pay you now? – all of that was washed away in 10 seconds.

They didn't even hear the whine that filled the room, almost like keening in its shrillness and persistence. They didn't hear the gargle it descended into as my vocal cords banged against each other, clamoring, desperately for purchase to let out the violent scream my mind had already loosed. Phlegm, mucus, fear, and confusion met at the back of my throat and sat there, choking me as the death rattle resounded in my office.

But they didn't hear it.

What they heard was my heavy breathing as she crawled near, then stood before me in a movement too quick for the eye to see. They heard the hitch in my breathing as it caught on the intake, nearly stopping in my throat as she stood before me with a razor-toothed grin and eyes as dark as space.

A starless night.

Pitch black and cold... so very cold.

She cocked her head as I regarded her, my breathing shallow now. The bastard running the conference bridge had called my name once, twice, three times before finally putting my line on mute. Apparently there was too much noise - some kind of rustling or windy interference, he called it - coming from my line.

Yeah, I guess so. Sorry to disturb you... just dying over here.

Her hand closed around my neck, which made the sounds worse. The gasping, choking sounds I gave out then would have definitely gotten me banned from the call had they heard them. I could hear my heartbeat in my ears, beating like a drum as the blood rushed pointlessly through my veins. My chest was tight, nothing more than a clenched fist that gathered all the muscles and ligaments and fibrous tissue in a pinch, constricting movement, constricting every-thing. I tried to breath and the pinch got tighter, a Charlie horse that would drop a runner to their knees, but inside my fucking chest.

Tight.

Restricting.

Killing.

The apples of her cheeks rose, making her bottomless pit eyes smile at the corners. It was grotesque and it made my eyes water. Or maybe the lack of oxygen did. Or maybe it was the cramp that was more like the slash of a knife in my chest.

No, it was none of those, I knew as I heard the strained moan in my inner ear, the sound that never made it out of my open, gasping mouth. As her lips pressed against mine, the very moment that her cold, dead tongue licked into my mouth to spread its viscous black mucus around, I knew exactly what made my tears fall and wet the dirty hair of my unkempt beard.

I read an article that said we can hear after we die. All the sounds of grief from loved ones sitting at your bedside, the doctors cursing under their breath and medical staff running around trying to save you in flashy television drama fashion – they say you can hear all of that even after your heart has stopped beating. Consciousness in the first phase of death, they called it, and I'm here to tell you that they are 100% correct, only I didn't hear anyone pronouncing my time of death nor was there sobbing because my life had ended or for the disposition of my immortal soul. Instead, I heard about the plans for a hotfix to be applied in the wee hours of the morning, one that would be done in addition to the previously scheduled emergency change, one that would fix the current problem but likely cause another... one whose go/no go conference bridge I would not be around for.

ABOUT THE AUTHOR

L. Marie Wood is an award-winning psychological horror author and screenwriter. She won the Golden Stake Award for her novel *The Promise Keeper* and Best Horror and Best Afrofuturism/Horror/Sci-Fi screenplay awards at several film festivals. An Active member of the HWA, Wood's short fiction has been published in *Slay: Stories of the Vampire Noire* and the Bram Stoker Finalist anthology, *Sycorax's Daughters*.

Learn more about her at www.lmariewood.com or join the discussion on Twitter at @LMarieWood1 or on Facebook at www.facebook.com/LMarieWood .

Made in the USA
Columbia, SC
27 May 2021

38278836R00061